WITH A SIDE OF VENGEANCE

KAIT GAMBLE

With a Side of Vengeance
ISBN # 978-1-83943-874-5
©Copyright Kait Gamble 2017
Cover Art by Posh Gosh ©Copyright November 2017
Interior text design by Claire Siemaszkiewicz
Totally Bound Publishing

Published in 2020 by Totally Bound Publishing, United Kingdom.

WITH A SIDE OF VENGEANCE

Dedication

For Rebecca.
Thanks for being such a wonderful editor!

Chapter One

Giselle Suttikul tramped across the hot sand, kicking the scalding grains out of her flip-flops as she single-mindedly stalked toward her prey.

"I'm telling you, I think I just saw them," she huffed into her phone.

"And I keep telling you, he's not worth it! Forget him and move on, Elle. Preferably onto someone big and handsome who can totally rocks your socks in bed."

Elle held her phone away from her face so she could look at it incredulously before pressing it to her ear again. "Do you ever have a thought that originates from a spot that's not between your thighs, Angie?"

"It's not my thighs I'm worried about. You need someone to sweep you off your feet. To ring your bell. If only for one night. You don't know how good this is for you! God, I wish you'd told me what you were doing so I would have come with you."

"I don't know how you can think that Greg leaving me is a good thing." Distracted, Elle stumbled on a rock and swore. "I'll call you back in a bit." Having her friend hounding her while she was pursuing her wayward fiancé somewhat covertly wasn't helping.

"You've got to realize, losing Mr. Boring is a good thing! Find yourself a local hottie and get under him! It's the best way to get over a breakup, seriously."

"That's got to be the worst advice you've ever given me."

"It's not! Now get your groove on! Do the nasty! Go to pound town! Slam the ham! Polish the porpoise!"

Can a call get any more embarrassing? Elle rolled her eyes. "Bye, Angie." Hanging up, she then shoved the phone back into her pocket.

When she should have been losing herself in the breathtaking scenery and absorbing the glorious Antiguan sunshine, Elle focused on the beach. Not the beauty of the shimmering blue water or pristine white sand but searching for a familiar figure.

What on earth had possessed her to get on a plane and fly around the world just so she would have definitive proof that her fiancé was indeed cheating on her? Not only was cheating but had left her?

Do I really need to see it in person? What kind of masochist am I?

All while she had been completely oblivious until after the fact.

Anger, shame and embarrassment combined into an acid that burned in her veins.

All that Elle knew for sure was that he was with another woman and she needed to see it with her own eyes. Then the next thing Elle knew, she had crossed the ocean and was checking into the same resort.

And now she would get him back.

Or she would murder him.

She wasn't quite clear on that point yet.

The one thing that Greg Henning needed to know was that no one cheated on Giselle Suttikul and got away with it.

Especially not for some wannabe model he had met on Instagram then traveled all the way to Antigua to meet.

Antigua!

He wasn't able to spare a moment to pick her up from the dentist when she'd had work done and needed his help, but for this blonde he'd fly around the world.

It was crazy. Who did that?

But if he was crazy, then she had to be just as insane for following him.

Cursing her impulsiveness, she stayed the course, determined to do what she was there to do. *See. Confront. Destroy.*

She had half-expected—hoped—that she would arrive to find it had all been a big misunderstanding. That this was a surprise for her benefit. All the sacrifices she had made for him over the years had been noticed. That she had meant something to him.

Everything fell away as she stumbled to a stop, staring up the beach to see what only could be described as Greg and his new love frolicking in the shallows.

Elle pulled out her phone and took a photo then sent it to her friends and his. They were right. He wasn't away on business. Instead of the dull trip that he had talked her out of because 'he didn't want to make her suffer through another boring business function', Greg was on a tropical island living it up with some other woman. While Elle had no clue. Not the slightest suspicion that he'd wanted out of their relationship.

Or that he had been in one with someone else at the same time.

In fact, up until a few weeks ago they'd been planning out their future together. At least, she'd been under the delusion that forever was where they were headed. Though when Elle thought about it, and she had at length on the flight over, she realized she had been the one making all the plans. He had just gone along with her.

Betrayal gnawed at her gut as she watched them. What pierced her with an inexplicable dagger to the heart was longing. By all accounts, they looked like a couple in love. Greg wasn't scowling. Far from it. The weight that had always seemed to have been dragging him down had been lifted. As much as she hated to admit it, he looked happier with the new woman than he ever had when he'd been with her.

If that wasn't enough, the other woman was gorgeous. Cascading blonde hair, a killer body that didn't have a single flaw Elle could see...

Stomach cramping, Elle wished she'd worn something more flattering than cut-off shorts and a T-shirt, but she had wanted to fly under the radar. The last thing she needed was to be spotted by them. She tugged the wide brim of the sun hat down farther, pushing the bug-eye sunglasses up at the same time with her other hand.

Her phone pinged with what were sure to be responses to the photo. Ignoring the impulse to deal with it, Elle shoved the device into the back pocket of her shorts. Right now, for better or for worse, she wanted to get a closer look at the woman who had replaced her.

With a callous heart, Eirik Mikkelsen sipped his drink as he watched Celina and the little bastard who she had run off with. To be completely honest, he felt absolutely nothing but the itching need for vengeance while he observed them.

He had already begun to tire of her only a month into their relationship. Her incessant chatter, her blatant self-absorption — it had all irritated him. He had been about to break it off with her, but Celina must have sensed it coming to have beat him to the punch.

On top of everything else she had done, that was just the icing on the cake. He was always the one to end things. No one walked out on him.

Ever.

He had been caught off guard when Celina had questioned him about his intentions toward her after having spent only a few weeks dating. To him, the question simply underscored that it was time for her to go — not that he'd said anything of the sort. Nor did he encourage her to think there was a long-term future for them. She obviously didn't want to wait around or try to change his mind.

So, without the quiet dignity his other lovers had possessed, Celina had walked out on him and had left a smoldering wreck in her wake.

Celina had preferred to get into an argument over their relationship in the middle of a dinner party, doing her best to shame him in her final attempt to lock him down. If she'd thought that embarrassment would get him to commit to her, she'd miscalculated. Greatly.

So, he had ended their relationship in front of everyone, after which she'd retaliated by stealing whatever she managed to grab on her way out.

The worth of what she'd taken was inconsequential, for the most part. A car, a sculpture, a painting and the few things he'd actually bought her meant nothing in comparison to the humiliation she tried to heap on him by getting someone to try to tank stock in his family's company.

When Eirik heard that she had hooked her claws into a new man and was now in Antigua, he couldn't help but follow with retribution on his mind.

When he'd first found out he wondered if she had hooked this guy after she left him or had they been carrying on for a while? Celina seemed like the type who would want a backup.

After reading through the reports from investigators who had retraced her steps for the past few months his hunch had been proven correct. She had already been working the new man even before they'd broken up.

Eirik had kept a close eye on them from the moment he'd arrived, even taking the villa next door to them, though they had yet to notice since the gap between villas was quite large. From all accounts, they looked like a typical couple on holiday. Relaxed. Blissful.

He finished his drink.

All that's going to change.

Her unwitting new man was going to find out exactly what kind of woman he was dealing with. Eirik imagined the little fool thought himself the luckiest man alive to have found himself a gorgeous woman like Celina. She'd probably clouded his mind with sex, something she had attempted to do to Eirik. And probably many others.

Eirik almost pitied him. The worm would soon find out that beneath the glamorous veneer was a grasping, devious snake. A woman out to get whatever she could without a care for the damage she left behind. Eirik was unwilling to allow her to wreak all that harm and let her get away with it.

Watching them now, so happy and sure that they were safe, Eirik wanted to crush them both.

So many scenarios flitted through his mind. How would he do it? Should he walk right up to them and confront her? Eirik didn't want to give her the satisfaction he knew she would find in convincing herself that he'd come for her. It would be easier to just let things take their natural course. Celina would show her true colors eventually, but he wasn't patient enough for that. Not right now.

He studied them a moment longer before looking at the file open on his tablet. There wasn't much to know about the new man she was with.

Greg Henning was a hedge fund manager. He led a completely regular life, from what Eirik could see. A regular and very dull life. He understood why someone like Greg would be enamored with Celina. She was beautiful and alluring and everything about the woman screamed sex. It was easy to envision that all she had needed do to convince him to manipulate stock prices was bat her lashes. A move so simple but with repercussions that might have ruined Eirik's family.

It was also well known that Henning had a long-term girlfriend whom he had all but abandoned for Celina.

Eirik lingered over the photo attached to the next file. *Giselle Suttikul.* The woman who smiled back was beautiful and petite, almost elfin, with hair dark as a summer night, flawless milky skin, dark, almond-shaped eyes and lush lips. He attributed her features to her being half-Asian on her father's side, who was apparently a blue-collar type who had married up. He and his wife, a British heiress, had one daughter who had been ignored somewhat but who had become a stellar cellist and who had dropped out of the limelight a few years ago, just when she had begun to gain a following.

He imagined it was Henning's influence that had changed her trajectory.

Destined for fame yet saddled with a louse.

At the very least she was free of him.

The longer Eirik stared at her face, the more intrigued he became. How did someone so lovely and talented get involved with a cretin like Henning in the first place? And to throw everything away for someone like him? It was a pity she had wasted so much time and aptitude.

Where would she be now?

While he scanned the scene once more, Eirik imagined her living up her newfound freedom. Maybe somewhere like this.

Wherever Giselle was, she was better off without Henning.

Especially now that Eirik had made it his mission to destroy him along with Celina.

He took a long deep breath of the sultry sea air. This was the perfect place to mix a little business and pleasure. Not only had it been a long time since he'd taken some time off, it had been even longer since he'd visited somewhere like this. All white sands, blue-green water and palm trees. Eirik wished it was possible for him to just kick back and relax.

Perhaps afterward.

He let his gaze drift toward the couple again. This time, however, he noticed a small figure making a beeline toward them. At first he thought it might be a teen, perhaps some member of staff at the resort showing up for their shift. But the way they seemed fixated on Celina and her man had him thinking otherwise.

The youth, obviously female from the way she moved, even pulled out a phone and took a photo or two of them before putting it away and continuing on her winding journey.

What is she up to?

Intrigued, Eirik put his drink down and headed down the path from his villa to follow the tracks in the sand.

What the hell am I doing? The anger and lust for vengeance evaporated the closer to them she got. She had flown all this way—tracked them down—and for what? Elle had seen for herself what kind of man Greg was. A loser. A louse. It was enough. She needed to get her head together and move on.

There was no stopping her feet from advancing, however.

The couple was close enough now that she could make out the gilded detail of the other woman's bikini, which was basically strips of cloth that were aspiring to be a bathing suit. As well as the satisfied grin on Greg's face.

They looked so…happy.

And something in her chest fractured a little more. Elle rubbed the heel of her hand against the hollow ache.

Why would she break that up? She wasn't some spiteful vengeance-seeking harpy. He'd found his happiness. She would do the same.

Or…bide her time and get them when they least expected. She had a mental image of her sashaying up to them, looking fabulous. Then she would crush his heart under her heel.

Maybe even with a new man in tow. One who was the complete opposite to him.

Happy with her new game plan, as fanciful as it was, Elle stopped and backed up, fully intending to leave them be and enjoy her brief stay. It wasn't often she came to a place like this and she needed to make the most of it, not waste all of her time on revenge.

Luckily, the happy couple was too besotted with each other to notice anything going on around them, least of all her.

Elle only managed a few steps before slamming into a solid body hard enough to knock her hat off. Big hands steadied her around the waist to help her regain her footing, but not before turning her around to face a wall-like chest. For several heartbeats, all she saw was a fading navy T-shirt stretched tight over muscle.

"Are you okay?"

The deep, only just accented voice drew her attention upward over the broad chest, the intriguing skin at the collar and the longish beard the color of wheat on a sunny day, to meet and hold his gaze. Elle stared in wonder into the pools of honey brown for much longer than she intended.

He looked as if someone had pulled a Viking out of the past and had barely managed to civilize him.

Although he had the beard, the features underneath were chiseled. To add to the look of barely tamed wildness, his hair was long and pulled back into a bun, one that her fingers itched to loosen. What would it look like? How long was it? Would it feel like silk in her fingers? She'd wager it would. His large hands warmed her through the thin T-shirt she wore, but with a shift of his fingers, the impersonal hold somehow changed into something else. His touch sent waves of heat to flare behind her belly button and had her imagining just how they would feel caressing the rest of her…

What the hell am I thinking?

Elle lurched back out of his grasp. Just her luck, his scent had wound itself around her and she couldn't escape the delicious fresh, woodsy aroma. She caught herself before she actually started licking her lips.

Snatching her hat off the sand, she stood to glare at him. "I'm fine. You shouldn't sneak up on people like that."

His lips tilted in a small smile. "I apologize."

Pulse fluttering at her throat, she nodded. "Apology accepted." When she meant to walk away, Elle found she wanted to stare into those golden eyes a moment longer. Wanted his hands back on her. Wanted to know what his skin tasted like.

It was insane. She'd never had such a visceral physical response to anyone in her life. And that it came from someone she would never have looked at twice was baffling.

She had a type, just like most people. Elle gravitated toward unassuming men who looked decent in a suit and were generally unthreatening. Completely unlike the man in front of her who, she imagined, was ready to pick up a sword right then and there and take on the world.

No matter what thoughts were unspooling in her mind, her body gravitated toward his.

Appalled, Elle took another deliberate step back.

Her Viking, however, had other ideas and took a step in tandem, mirroring her movement to perfection. Feeling like prey under his steady, almost predatory gaze, Elle stumbled back, prompting him to steady her once again.

This time, his hand closed around her wrist. She was positive he felt her pulse fluttering there in time with the rapid beat of her heart. She stared up at him while he peered down at her. Caught unprepared and completely overwhelmed by her reaction to him, Elle could only just force herself to breathe.

"Elle?"

The choked voice on the edge of panic broke the hazy trance and dragged Elle's attention away from the man holding her.

Greg must have been mid-fondle when he'd spotted her, because he and the woman were still wound around each other, locked mid-action. Even her leg was wrapped around his hip and her tongue still in his ear.

Elle swallowed back the bile that had propelled itself upward from her rolling stomach.

Greg nearly dropped the woman in his haste to step back and jog toward them. He stared at her at her with wide, frantic eyes. "What are you doing here?"

What to say? That she had tracked him here? That she hadn't been thinking when she'd gotten on a plane and flown over to see for herself that he had been cheating on her?

She was about to go on the offensive when another voice cut her off.

The words, "Elle is here with me," were uttered an instant before she was drawn into a solid chest.

Chapter Two

Eirik had recognized Henning's jilted lover when he'd still been half a beach away from her. As he'd gotten closer, her beauty on top of her reticence had become clearer and clearer. Even in her so-called disguise, it would have been easy to spot her from a mile away in a crowd of people.

The delicate scent of her, floral and feminine on the breeze, had enticed him closer. Until the next thing he'd known, she was only a breath away. Then when he'd reached her, the surge of lust that had prompted him to seek her out had smashed at the chains of his control. He'd had to touch her. To smell her. To taste her.

To claim her.

Seeing her falter under Henning's scrutiny had given him the perfect opportunity to save face for both of them.

He tugged her close and wound an arm comfortably around her waist. "Elle and I were enjoying some much-needed alone time together. Isn't that right, *elskling*?" He gazed down at her. Imagining she was his made a look of devotion all too easy to muster.

She was such a petite woman. Visions of how snug she would be around him seized his lungs, making him fight for a calming breath. She must have sensed the tension thrumming through him, because she leaned back to look up at him. For an instant she looked confused, then terrified. But, to her credit, it turned adoring in the blink of an eye.

Eirik lifted his gaze from her to let it fall on Celina. "It's a surprise to see you here."

Celina's reaction was much more controlled than Henning's. She made sure that her walk to Henning's side flaunted her assets. Or at least what she thought were her best features. He hadn't been overly fond of her implants, above the waist or below.

The trembling woman pressed to his side, however, fit against him like a missing puzzle piece. And what he felt of her was enough to have him fighting the urge to peel off her clothing to see if it all looked as good as it felt.

"I'm not surprised to see you in the least. I should have known that you would wait to follow me, but the result is the same in the end. Here you are." The gloating tone was made more clear in her eyes and smirking smile.

Though the implication that he'd followed her because he still wanted her hung in the air like a sour note, he wasn't going to bite. There would be plenty of time to tear her to shreds later. Right now, he wanted to get to know Elle and formulate some sort of plan that would appease his need for retribution for them both.

There was no helping the smile that spread across his face when Elle closed her arms around him the best she could and burrowed closer. He had no way to be absolutely sure, but Eirik thought he'd heard—and felt—her inhaling deeply enough to fill her lungs while her face had been pressed to his chest.

He grinned at the other couple before lowering his gaze lovingly at Elle. "Nice to see you, but we need to get going." The insinuation was clear. They wanted to be alone.

And from the puckered expression Celina's face assumed, she didn't like it.

"Elle?" Henning, however, was still floundering. "Aren't you going to introduce us?"

Eirik stepped in before Elle revealed she had no idea who he was. "Is this a friend of yours, *elskling*?" He waved the question away and addressed Henning. "Celina will fill you in, I'm sure. Elle and I are in a bit of a rush." He gave him a look that he hoped would impress upon Henning that he was cock-blocking.

From the gaping look he received in return, the other man did and was at an utter loss.

Not giving anyone a chance to say anything more, Eirik led Elle back toward his villa.

Only, the farther away from the other couple they got, the more agitated Elle became until they were only a few steps away from the staircase hewn from the stone rising from the beach to his temporary home.

He didn't try to hold onto her when she pulled away, though his instinct was to do so.

She backed away from him, nibbling on her bottom lip at the same time. "Thanks for that, but I'm not going anywhere with you."

"You're welcome." He kept his voice even and mild, not wanting to scare her off. "And I only thought we should get to know each other since we seem to have so much in common."

That seemed to confuse her further. "He left me for her. So what?"

"And she left me for him. I think that gives us quite a bit to talk about." Putting on his most charming smile, he held out his hand. "Why don't you come up and we'll do so over dinner?"

Elle stared, clearly trying to figure him out.

"I swear I'm not a serial killer or anything." He put up his hand. "Dinner and conversation. That's it."

Seeming to fight a silent inner war, she relaxed a little after a moment though the wary light in her eyes hadn't dimmed.

She placed her hand in his. "Okay. I'll have dinner with you, but at one of the restaurants." She looked down the beach at the one in the distance to make her point.

She was cautious, at least. Eirik smiled. "But that would bring us back past a pair of people I think we'd both rather avoid right now."

Elle frowned, but he saw she was after some answers, because she sighed, "Fine. Dinner at your villa."

His smile grew as he waved her toward the stairs.

She had to be out of her mind. It had to be due to what Greg had done. Before all this, she never would have considered going to a virtual stranger's villa. Or let him hold her and use her to needle his ex.

Or wonder what being kissed by him would feel like…

Elle wrenched her mind back on track. So their exes were together now. What a great thing to have in common between them.

Why couldn't they have met in some wildly romantic fashion like people did in the movies? Like eyes catching across the room or getting tangled up in dog leashes? Granted, she didn't have a dog, but it had always been a fantasy of hers to have a man just look at her and fall madly in love and vice versa.

She watched him order from one of the restaurants on the resort. She knew this because on the flight over she'd read with wide-eyed wonder about all the available amenities and wished she'd had the funds to try them all. The restaurants and spas especially. At least now she'd get a tiny taste from one. A small consolation.

Elle brought her focus back to the man in the room with her. Tall, handsome, larger than life. Who would be crazy enough to leave this man? Unless…he was damaged beyond repair, somehow?

Sure, Greg had been a safe choice, but in comparison to the man in front of her, Greg wasn't much. Shorter by several inches, less muscled. Less…everything, if she was being honest. But physical dominance was nothing. Greg might not have had his name in lights, but he was a decent man.

At least she had thought so until he'd dumped her without warning…after cheating on her…

She mulled over that thought during her scan of the room. This villa was much more opulent than her own, not at all a surprise. She'd had to make due with a tiny shack crammed together with many others, which had cost more than she cared to think about, where his was huge, airy and with its own section of the beach. It must have cost him a fortune to rent. What she wouldn't give to stay somewhere like this for a little while.

Her attention was drawn back to her host as he sat down across from her. Ratty T-shirt, jeans faded and soft from wear, bare feet. If he hadn't brought her to this villa, she would have figured him for a beachcomber with a hut on the beach somewhere.

By all evidence, that would have been a very, very wrong assumption.

His smile was open, charming. "I hope you don't mind—I ordered for the both of us."

Elle had hated it when Greg ordered for her. For the most part because he'd almost always got it wrong, but she wasn't going to labor her position right now. What was the point? She probably wouldn't eat a thing, anyway.

"That's fine." She eyed him, waiting for him to say something, but when he didn't, Elle sighed. "So are you going to at least tell me your name?"

He studied her a moment, making her feel as if he was delving into her soul with those stunning eyes of his. "I'm Eirik Mikkelsen."

He held his hand out and she took it after staring at it for a full second. Her hand was engulfed right away in his, sending a zap of electricity up her arm. For a moment she let herself revel in the feel of his skin against hers. "Giselle Suttikul."

"A pleasure." His smile was genuine and he didn't seem ready to let her hand go, instead keeping hold of it. "I'm sure you have a lot of questions about what just happened."

"You can say that again."

He released her hand, letting it slide out of his as if with reluctance, and settled back. "I want revenge on them."

Well, that was blunt. And oddly in line with her own motives for being there in the beginning. "You think that's a good use of your time?"

His expression grew curious. "Isn't that why you're here?"

"Maybe when I first got here." She shrugged. "Don't you think we should just let bygones be bygones?"

"No." He leaned back in his chair and regarded her with careful scrutiny. "I think they should pay for what they've done."

Elle shook her head. "So she hurt your pride a little. So what? You'll have a new girlfriend on your arm in a matter of days, I'm sure." That thought unsettled something in her. Why did the idea of him being with someone else make her stomach roll?

The corners of his lips curled up in amusement while he gave her a considering gaze. "Perhaps. But that doesn't excuse what she did. It's more than a matter of pride. She tried to ruin not only me and my name but my family's. With the help of your ex, I might add."

Still skeptical, she frowned. "What do you think they did?"

"They worked together to manipulate stock prices in an attempt to ruin my family's company."

She felt the color drain from her face. "What?" Elle shook her head again. "That can't be. Greg wouldn't do that."

"Wouldn't he? Why would I lie?" Eirik leaned forward, bracing his sculpted forearms on his knees. "Look at it this way. Did you not also think that he would be faithful?"

Eirik was right about that. What did she really know about Greg? Judging from what he'd done and what Eirik said he'd done, not much.

"Maybe I was wrong about him, but what can we do about it?"

"I propose we work together to make them regret ever messing with us."

Part of her was intrigued while the rest of her just wanted to go to sleep for the next month. "I don't know if that's such a good idea."

His strong jaw dropped a little. "You don't want vengeance?"

"I'm not saying that." *What* am *I saying?* Her head was spinning. "I'm just really tired and I've been through a lot in the past few days. I can't think straight. Can we at least leave the plotting until after we've eaten?"

A smile spread over his face at the fact that she wasn't turning him down outright. "Very well."

"Great. Now I'm going to rest my eyes for a minute." Elle wished for the luxury to curl up on the comfortable sofa and go to sleep. Instead, she slid into the corner and leaned her head back, fully intending to keep one eye open to watch him. She was just so comfortable... As her eyes drifted closed, a breeze whispered over her, bringing with it the exotic scents of Antigua and the intriguing whiff of male. When she opened her eyes a crack, she spied Eirik across the room next to an opened balcony door.

That was considerate of him.

The cooling air was just what she needed to both relax and be refreshed.

She closed her eyes again and waited for the food to arrive.

Eirik stood at the glass doors, but rather than look out at the scenery, his gaze was drawn to the woman on the couch. Her delicate features did indeed look tired, but it didn't distract him from her beauty. To get her into bed and get revenge on Celina and Henning would make this trip perfection.

The longer he gazed at her, however, the less important the non-Elle parts of the plan became. In fact, he could think of nothing better to do right now than watch her.

Relaxed in pseudo-sleep, she was even more striking. Her face was smooth and unmarred by stress or fatigue. With her eyes closed, her long lashes dusted her cheeks. There was evidence of how tired she was in the dark circles under them. Eirik let his gaze travel along her fine cheekbones, down a long and graceful neck, over a pair of pert breasts and down a lean body then back up to take her all in again. *Exquisite.* Even her fingers were elegant.

She definitely merited better than that idiot Henning.

Elle needed someone who would appreciate her. Treat her the way she deserved. To show her just how good it could be between a man and a woman.

Someone like him.

The knock at the door halted the thoughts. He crossed the room and opened the door, allowing a mini retinue of waiters carrying dome-covered trays of varying sizes in.

By the time they had the meal set up on the table on the balcony, Elle was up and wandering over.

He tipped them and let them make their own way out. Eirik pulled free a chair for her. While she settled into her seat, he opened the wine and filled their glasses. "I hear the food from this particular restaurant is incredible."

"It smells fantastic." She reached for one of the domes. "May I?"

"Of course." Watching for her reaction, he took his seat. "I wasn't sure what you would like so I got a bit of everything. They specialize in seafood, however. I hope that's to your liking."

"*A bit?*" Elle's eyes widened when she lifted one dome after another while he revealed what was hidden on the trays closest to him.

Shrimp, lobster, steak, chicken, salads, grilled vegetables... There had to be something there to tempt her.

Elle sniffed the aromas and sighed happily. "Perfect."

To his surprise, it pleased him that she thought so. "Help yourself."

She proceeded to take bits of just about everything, leaving a large portion for him. Once done, she waited for him to take what he liked. Polite, considerate. So far Elle wasn't lacking in looks or manners. Still, there had to be something more than Celina's false charms that had prompted the other man to leave Elle.

He wanted to know whether Henning was a complete idiot or perhaps she was a nightmare to be with. Musicians were reputed to be temperamental. Maybe she was a terror once she let her guard down?

Eirik watched her as she waited for him, even though it was evident she was famished.

Somehow he doubted that she would be a shrew. So what would prompt Henning to leave someone like her?

He picked up his glass and held it out to her. "To new friends."

Friends? Elle wouldn't call them that, though her unruly body clamored to be more than.

She was just tired and hungry. Once she got herself sorted out, she'd see things with a more impartial eye. *That's what it is. Low blood sugar.*

Tapping the rim of her glass to his, she kept her thoughts to herself. After taking a quick sip, Elle put it back on the table eager to sample the sumptuous-looking food.

What didn't escape her notice was that they both started with the scrumptious lobster. Elle sighed with delight the moment the morsel touched her tongue. So good. Each mouthful was more delicious than the last. She couldn't remember the last time she'd eaten anything so wonderful.

Or it might have been so good because of the company.

Eirik didn't say much, preferring to enjoy his meal and let her enjoys hers. It was nice. The companionable silence was pleasant, especially when compared to the chatter that Greg had liked to fill the quiet with. He'd never seemed comfortable just enjoying a peaceful moment together.

She did, however, feel Eirik's silent regard. Not that she wasn't guilty of the same. Try as she might, it was hard to keep her eyes off him. In addition to being handsome, he was enigmatic. There was a brooding quality about him, a quiet strength, that Elle found herself drawn to.

There was also what he said about what his ex and Greg had done. While it was awful, it had been the most intriguing thing she'd heard in a long time. In fact, this entire situation was more interesting than anything she'd ever been involved in.

Peeking at her dining companion through her lashes, Elle decided to break the silence. "Can you tell me more about what you think Greg and your ex did?"

"I don't *think*. I know." Eirik sat back, taking his glass of wine with him. Gazing at her over the rim, he took an indolent sip.

"Well?" Elle waited and mimicked him. She let the flavor of the wine burst on her tongue, waiting for him to explain.

He smirked. "Celina had been dropping some not so subtle hints that she wanted things to become more permanent between us."

Typical. "So you kicked her to the curb? No wonder she flipped out. The poor woman." Elle imagined how devastating it would be to be loved then discarded by this man. She rubbed away the goosebumps from her arms.

Eirik noticed straight away. "Would you like to move indoors?"

She shook her head. "You were saying? You broke this woman's heart…"

A husky huff of air burst from his lips. "Broke her heart? Hardly. She doesn't love me. Never did. Celina's more interested in my family's wealth."

That wasn't so surprising. Though it was so typical that it aroused her suspicion. "I'm supposed to take your word for it?"

"I would be disappointed if you did, but if you would just give me the benefit of the doubt for the moment?"

Elle could. For now. "Okay. So she's a mercenary gold digger who's tried to bring you down after you dumped her. You're telling me she recruited Greg to help her do this?"

"I have proof."

He sounded so sure. Elle doubted Eirik was the type of man to throw around accusations without something to back them up.

Eirik go up and disappeared for a moment before returning with a tablet. "All the proof you need is on here." He flicked through files then presented her with the device. "Feel free to go through it all."

Taking a slow breath, Elle took it from him and placed it next to her. "I'll read it after we eat, if that's okay."

He nodded, prompting her to drink another sip of her wine. "Say I believe you. That everything is there in black and white. What do you think you can do about it? Neither of them wants us anymore, so why bother with the theatrics? Just take it to the authorities."

"He humiliated you. Don't you want vengeance?"

"I did, until I got here and saw how happy he was with her. It's more than he ever was with me."

Eirik looked unimpressed. "So, you would let him get away with hurting you."

When he put it that way, how could she feel anything but a little embarrassed? Anger flared. Why should she let him make her feel…anything?

Elle put the glass down. "I'm not letting him get away with anything. I'm choosing to be the bigger person and getting on with my life. He can do whatever he wants with his. He's no longer my problem." She pushed herself back from the table to stand. "Thank you for dinner. It was lovely, but I think it's time I left. Good luck with getting your revenge."

He mirrored her actions and caught up with her to open the door. "If you're telling me that you're not the least bit interested in hurting him back, that's fine. I'll do my best not to involve you in the fallout."

"Great. Thanks," she deadpanned.

Why was his easy dismissal so upsetting? Elle didn't expect him to ask her to stay, but once the door was open and she was free to go, she wanted to spend more time with him. To find out more about him. To try to figure him out.

To just stare at Eirik a little longer.

Pushing aside the pathetic thought with a sigh, Elle turned and was about to bid him goodbye when he put his hand on her shoulder. Her breath caught at the torrent of sensation pinballing through her from his touch.

"Except they've already seen us together..." His voice was soft, cajoling. "No matter what happens now, they'll assume you're a part of it."

Elle's stomach dropped. "Are you blackmailing me?"

"That's such an ugly word and not what I'm doing at all." He smiled, giving her a dose of his dangerous charm, and stepped closer. So close that the heat emanating from him warmed her. "I'm just pointing out the obvious."

What was obvious to Elle was that she wasn't going to be getting away from this man any time soon.

And, strangely enough, she was perfectly okay with that.

Chapter Three

Eirik saw the moment he had her. Her face, especially her eyes, was so expressive that it wasn't at all difficult to discern. It would be hard for her to hide any emotion from anyone who was paying attention. And he intended to pay very close attention.

Not that it would be any hardship. Spending time with Elle, brief though it had been, was pleasant. She was smart and kind — or was it naïve — enough to let a long-time lover walk away without a fight after seeing him happy with someone else.

Eirik, on the other hand, wasn't so generous.

He wanted Celina and Henning to suffer. Using Elle to do it would be icing on the cake. He'd get revenge and a pleasurable vacation at the same time. Two birds with one truly fetching stone.

There was nothing more delightful to him than when a plan came together.

But first he had to convince the wide-eyed woman on the couch to play along.

Easy.

She watched him with big, cautious brown eyes, but he saw something else in their depths as well. Elle was interested in him. He recognized that spark even when she tried to hide it.

That would work very well in his favor.

Eirik led her to the balcony again, but this time situated them at the railing to watch the undulating waves. The hope was that the scenery would instill a sense of peace in her as the sea always did for him.

The darkening sky stretched into the distance with ribbons of blues and purples, dipping into the horizon and blending into the inky water like it was drawing the darkness of it into the heavens. The breeze cooled while it soothed with its tantalizing mix of exotic scents.

Inhaling the mingled tang of the sea and tropical flowers, he turned to the woman who was still staring up at him as if she didn't quite believe what she was looking at.

"Is something wrong?"

Elle jumped a little. Had she not realized what she was doing?

He smiled. "Want another glass of wine? Or something else, perhaps? I can call up for anything you like."

She took half a second to think about it then shook her head. "No. Thank you." Elle turned to stare out at the water with a haunted look on her face.

"What are you thinking?"

"So many things."

He turned so his back was against the railing to face her. "Tell me. We have nothing but time here."

She met his gaze again. Held it this time. "I feel like I'm about to get used."

Eirik approved of her candor. He would do the same...to a point. "More than Henning used you?"

Her back straightened. "He and I were in a relationship."

As if that excused anyone using their partner in any way. "Not much of one if how easy it was for him to walk away is anything to go by."

Pain flashed in her eyes and he caught the glimmer of tears before she blinked them away. Not good enough, he needed her angry. *Vengeful.*

"As I see it, he used you in the worst way a man could and you're just going to let him get away with it." Eirik watched her, observing her reactions. Waiting for her to bite.

Bristling, she seemed to grow an inch. "What's it to you if I am? You don't know me. You have nothing to do with me."

He put up his hands. Her gaze was drawn to them. Interesting. "Hey, I'm in the same boat as you. I just thought since our problems seems to have a lot of the same people involved, we could help each other out."

She thought about that for a spell. "So what do you see us doing to get your revenge on them?"

"I'm sure something will come to me."

She gaped at him and for several seconds resembled a goldfish while she put together a reply. "You don't even have a plan?"

He shrugged. "I'm working on it." Movement on the beach nearby caught his attention.

Elle huffed a breath. "All this fuss and you haven't even got a plan."

"I have the beginnings of one." He edged closer, prompting her to move back a little. Eirik shifted closer again. "For example, I see our exes just over there right now. Don't look." He tugged on her hands to keep her attention focused on him.

Pursing her lips, she gazed up at him. "So what do we do?"

"This."

Eirik lowered his head and brushed his lips against hers.

Elle stood frozen as he gave her the lightest ghost of a kiss. But before registering what was happening, scorching heat flared between them and the kiss turned into a hotter, biting parody of the innocent touching of mouths. In that moment, kissing Eirik was more important than anything else that was going on. Breathing was a secondary concern. That Greg would see them didn't even register.

All Elle knew was that she wanted more of Eirik. His taste. His touch...

What the hell am I doing?

Elle tried to escape his grasp, but Eirik held her tight, continuing his plunder of her mouth before pulling back for a breath and to growl, "Make them believe it."

What did it matter if they believed it or not? Elle couldn't believe she was there, kissing a man she'd known mere hours as though her life depended on it.

So he wants to give them a show, does he?

Elle gave into the impulse to link her arms around his neck. She hauled herself up to capture his mouth. Pressed herself closer until she felt every hard angle of his body through their clothing. It was only because she wasn't sure what to do with her legs that she didn't wrap them around his hips to get closer.

Eirik closed his hands around her waist, scooping one under her bottom, picking her up and holding her tighter to him in one move.

Changing the angle of the kiss, Elle reveled in the feel of him so hard and strong against her. When his hand crept up under her shirt, she smiled against his lips, gasping when the slightly rough rasp of his hand climbed higher.

She found herself placed on the edge of the railing, allowing him the use of both hands. Inch by inch, he rucked up the thin fabric. The rush of the cool breeze over her skin was in stark contrast to the heat flaring from his touch.

The frustrating thing was, he stopped just below her bra. Teasing at the hem — nudging the underwire — but never straying upward. Elle moaned her exasperation into his mouth, prompting a chuckle from him.

Eirik gave her a nipping kiss before drawing back to gaze at her with heavy-lidded eyes.

Fighting for air and trying to comprehend what had just happened, Elle forced every emotion, every sensation he'd coaxed from her back down. But not before licking her lips to get one last taste of him.

It took her a few breaths before she managed a whispered, "Think they bought it?"

He only smiled at her as he helped her back down from the railing and set her on her feet.

With her knees wobbling, she let him lead her into the villa, curious what would happen now.

Eirik still tasted her on his lips when he picked up the bottle of wine and poured two glasses. The kiss had shaken him a little. More than a little, if he was being honest with himself. From a glance at her, she wasn't quite steady either.

Fighting the urge to drop everything and kiss her again, he handed Elle a glass then sat next to her. Not touching, but close enough to wrap an arm around her if the need came.

The emotions flitting across her face were incredible to watch. Everything was there. Lust, excitement, confusion, self-loathing, fear — all mingled with sleepy pleasure. He'd wager that the savage power of the kiss had been something new for her, too.

Her hand trembled when she raised the glass, though it eased a little when she lowered it to glare at him. "Aren't you going to say something?"

"I want to kiss you again."

He caught the quick intake of breath before she peeked her tongue out from between her lips to swipe over her lower one.

Eirik knew he had to tread lightly. "I won't. Not without your permission. But I do want to." More than he wanted to admit.

She breathed a little easier, though the tension in her small body was clear. "It was a good kiss."

"Very good."

At least she agreed with that. So now what? He knew he wanted to explore whatever this was, at least until he got it out of his system.

"I was thinking that you should stay here." He caught her shocked gaze. "As part of the ruse. There are three bedrooms besides the master suite. You can have your pick."

She blinked a few times before she managed to formulate an argument. "I doubt they'll notice if I'm not here all the time."

Eirik shrugged. "They might, considering they have the villa next door."

Smoothing out the slight crease between her eyebrows, Elle sighed. "Fine. But I want your assurance that you'll give me my space."

"Of course."

She didn't look quite convinced, but she didn't seem to have much else to say. In fact, she was looking quite wilted.

Still, Eirik took it as a small victory.

"Shall I have someone bring your things?"

There was a negligent lift of her shoulders which he took to be affirmation.

"Why don't you take a bath? The bathrooms are fully stocked."

"All right." Elle pushed herself up from the couch and looked to him for direction.

"That way." He pointed down the hall. "To the left, you'll find the spare rooms. Each one has its own en suite."

"Thanks."

Her listlessness triggered concern. "Are you okay?"

"Just super."

Elle followed his directions and soon found herself in an incredible room that overlooked the ocean, with her own balcony equipped with chaise, chairs and table. She didn't need to look at any of the others. This one would do.

It took a lot of willpower not to throw herself onto the bed to see if it was as soft as it looked. She was grimy from a long day. The last thing she wanted to do was get sand on it. Instead, Elle wandered past the huge closet and the mirror's vanity, catching a glimpse of herself.

She stopped dead and raked a hand through her hair. No wonder he'd suggested a bath. She looked terrible.

And yet he'd kissed her.

Then pretty much let her down. With gentle care and consideration. But it had still hurt to be rejected by him after such an incredible kiss.

It wasn't like she'd never been kissed before. The ones she'd shared with Greg had always been nice. Pleasant at best. The astonishing, knee-knocking variety, she'd thought a myth. Until today.

Elle walked into the bathroom and had to stop for a moment to take in the sheer opulence of it. All glass and rough stone, it looked natural while at the same time she knew immense time and expense had gone into its engineering. Just like the rest of the resort.

She kicked off her sandals first, then her shorts. Elle ignored the large bathtub and walked to the huge glass enclosure and turned on the huge overhead shower. Eager to get under the spray, she tore off her shirt and underwear, dropping them with the rest of the discarded clothing.

There was no better shower experience in her memory, but the entire time in it was spent licking her wounds. In the span of a few weeks, she'd been rejected by two men. One after knowing her for years and the other after a few hours.

The resulting feeling of isolation and rejection mingled in a cold ball at the bottom of her gut. Maybe if she was different, they wouldn't have been put off by her?

Eirik might have said that he wanted to kiss her again, but he hadn't. She knew it was ridiculous and that he was probably just being a decent man, but it had still stung.

Just once, she wished she had a man who wanted her with such single-minded fervor that he'd give up everything for her. Like how Greg was with Celina.

Maybe she just didn't inspire that in men?

Whatever it was, Elle was left feeling dejected and deflated.

All she wanted to do was get some sleep so she could regain her perspective on things.

She used the contents of the bottles one by one and was soothed by the effects and the decadent scents.

The enormous fluffy towels were a treat to use. By the time she exited the bathroom, she felt semi-human again. But bone tired.

It was time to put the horrible day to rest.

On her bed were the tablet and her only bag, a backpack that she had crammed with a few essentials before catching the flight. Pitiful really. It was clear that Eirik had brought it in and seen how little she had with her. Not only that, but he still expected her to read through his proof.

Wonderful.

She dug through for another, larger T-shirt she'd had the foresight to pack. It wasn't until she had slipped it on that she noticed a note on her pillow.

The script was clean, economic. There wasn't a wasted stroke to form the words.

Sleep well. I'll see you in the morning. Eirik.

That was nice of him. Or maybe he just didn't want to see her face again that night?

Elle shrugged it all away. She didn't care. She wouldn't allow herself to. All she wanted was to get in that bed and sleep for the next month.

Only sleep wouldn't come.

For what felt like hours, all Elle saw when she closed her eyes was Greg and Celina on the beach. And when she wasn't thinking about that, her mind kept circling back to the blistering kiss she'd shared with Eirik. Which in turn made her body throb in reaction.

Frustrated and aching, Elle found it impossible to relax enough to fall asleep.

Rather than waste the night tossing and turning in the bed, Elle opted to get up and open the door to her balcony for some fresh air. She might as well make use of everything the island had to offer while she was able.

Taking her phone and Eirik's tablet with her, she stepped out onto the cool wooden deck, enjoying the feel of the grain against the soles of her feet. The pleasantly chilled night air carried with it the tantalizing bite of the sea. She settled onto the chaise and let the steady cadence of the waves lull her into a sense of tranquility. Or at least the closest to it she'd get at the moment.

The cool breeze felt wonderful on her heated skin and the chaise so comfortable. If only she had gone and found some wine and maybe a snack…

Too late now.

Elle tilted her head back to stare at the heavy sprinkling of stars in the velvety sky overhead. A magnificent view that she never would have seen from a light-polluted city. She gazed in wonder at the heavens.

She had no idea how long she spent doing just that, but for the sense of calm that it brought her, it would have been worth lying there all night.

Elle let her attention wander to the architecture of the building. Even in the dim light, she had to admire the craftsmanship and work that had gone into the design.

The balcony seemed to wrap around the building to be shared by the other rooms as well. Probably to facilitate a family or group of friends, so they didn't feel segregated. It was a lovely building and a great design for it. It fit the surroundings perfectly. As did the others that dotted the beach in soft pools of light.

And yet there wasn't much pleasure she took in it.

Closing her eyes only brought back her turmoil. Greg and Celina frolicked in her mind, reminding her that all the things she'd heard about him were true. There was no hiding her head in the sand any longer. Greg had left her and had probably been cheating on her for months.

How could she not want some retribution for that?

Then there were all the things that Eirik said Greg had done for his new woman...

With a sense of impending dread, she picked up the tablet and turned it on.

Like Eirik said, it was all there. She didn't need to be a financial genius to figure it out though there were so many pages that it had all started to run together by the time she put the tablet down. What she gathered was that Greg had set up numerous dummy accounts to buy up stock in Mikkelsen Engineering Inc. The interest caught the eye of others and soon others were buying up the hot shares.

Now she figured he was poised to start selling, which would send the stock prices plummeting. It was reprehensible. Had Eirik's ex put him up to it or had he come up with it all by himself to show off for her? Whatever the reason, he was an idiot and Eirik had everything in his possession to take him down.

It was a miracle Eirik had caught him before things went very badly for his family's business and for what was probably hundreds if not thousands of people employed by them.

No wonder he was so furious.

She found more files in the folder that linked Celina with Greg. Eirik had been very thorough in his pursuit of them. There were photos, detailed reports with dates and times of every little interaction…

It was all very damning.

With all the new evidence, Elle had to admit that Eirik had the right idea. But did she want to work with someone like him? And just how far was he willing to go for his revenge?

What was he like? For the short time she'd known him, Elle knew that he was vengeful, goal-oriented. Handsome as sin…

And his kisses…

And there was the fact that Eirik was right. It would be an injustice if Greg got away with doing this to her and most certainly what he tried to do to Eirik.

After everything she'd given up for Greg. The things she had put aside so that she would be more free for him. This was how he repaid her?

She was the idiot for having gone along with it in the first place. Tears blurred her vision. Taking deep, slow breaths, Elle tried again to let the smooth rhythm of the waves sooth her. The slow, steady beat brought to mind a composition she had worked on years ago but hadn't had the time to finish.

Even after so long, the melody — faint as it was — still echoed in her head.

Taking solace in that, she let the music come together. One note after another, whirling around inside her.

It felt wonderful to just let the music flow and not have to worry about missing a call from Greg or having to go to a party with his colleagues. Or one of the hundreds of other things that she 'should' be doing instead.

Letting her tears flow along with the imaginary music, she wished she had her cello or something to write it down on.

Just when the music reached a crescendo in her mind, her phone pinged with a text alert. She didn't know what had made her bring it out with her, though she knew that she should check in with Angie or she'd think she was dead. She'd be worried if she stayed silent too long.

But when she saw that the latest text had come from Greg, Elle's blood pressure threatened to pop her head like an overheated thermometer.

Instead, she opted to get the reminder of him as far away from her as possible and launched her phone into the night.

* * * *

There was no way Eirik was getting any sleep after that kiss. Knowing Elle was so close yet out of reach wreaked havoc with his imagination. With his body. It would have been so easy to just walk into her room and persuade her to open up to him. To give him everything.

But she needed time. She'd been hurt. They'd only just met. He needed her to stick around so they could get back at their exes. There were a dozen reasons for him to give her space.

But damned if he didn't want to pick up from where they left off earlier.

And that was how he found himself going for a jog along the beach in the middle of the night. The hope had been that the pent-up energy would be burned off with a stint of self-flagellation. To his dismay, it hadn't worked.

He briefly entertained the thought of running the beach again, for the fourth time, but it wasn't likely to make any difference.

The lust for Elle would still be there. Unabated and all-consuming.

And frustrating as hell.

He didn't have time for this. What he needed to be doing was figuring out how to redeem himself in his family's eyes. This mess with Celina had been the last in a line of stupid and humiliating choices that had added to the reputation of him being the family wastrel. Of course, he'd had to get involved with her just when he'd been working to rebuild his image.

The last thing he needed was to become embroiled with another woman. Even one as beguiling as Elle.

Eirik turned back toward the villa, prepared to suffer through the next few restless hours. Maybe a swim would help cool him off.

As he got closer, his attention zeroed in on her room on instinct.

He should check on her. Make sure she was okay. Elle seemed quite upset earlier.

Eirik stopped dead in his tracks. And now he was acting like a lovestruck boy trying to catch a glimpse of the object of his crush.

Even the blanket on the chaise outside on her balcony looked like her to his addled mind.

And moved like her…

It *was* Elle. What had prompted her to come out in the dark of night?

He quickly regained his pace.

Eirik cleared the steps three at a time and rounded the building, following the balcony around to her.

And just missed getting hit in the head by a dark projectile. It was only due to luck and his good reflexes that he managed to swipe it out of its trajectory, sending it flying into the night.

What the hell?

What was she throwing things at him for?

It wasn't until he got closer that he realized she hadn't even noticed his approach.

Elle stared at the ocean but didn't seem to see a thing. Whatever emotion she was caught up in had her completely in its grasp. The shine of tears on her cheeks eroded away the last vestige of his determination to stay away.

He stepped closer, careful to make enough noise so she knew he was approaching. She jolted when she realized she wasn't alone and swiped away the tears.

"Elle? I'm sorry to disturb you, but I was out running and saw you. Are you okay?"

She shook her head, sending her hair cascading over her shoulders. "Not really. I read the files on your tablet." Elle turned her big eyes to him in concern. "I didn't wake you, did I?"

She's concerned for me? Elle was too sweet to be real.

Shaking his head, he pointed at the shorts and running shoes. "I was burning off some pent-up energy with a run."

"Your ex must have upset you pretty badly, huh?"

"I'm more concerned about what she attempted to do. But you've read it now. You understand." He caught the fatigue in her eyes behind the sadness. He had to be made of stone not to be affected by it. "Since neither one of us is destined to get any sleep tonight, why don't we have some coffee?"

"Sure."

She took his proffered hand and didn't protest when he held onto it on the way to the living area.

"Want something to eat?"

Elle nodded.

Eirik didn't like the blank, haunted look in her eyes. The urge to wipe the wounded hollowness out of them surprised him. He wanted to take care of her though he barely knew her.

Uncustomary doubt nagged his decision to invite her to stay with him.

Shoving the unsettling emotion aside, he focused on finding something to eat. Making the coffee was quick and easy. Finding food was just as simple thanks to a fully stocked fridge. Within minutes he had coffee, bottles of mineral water, bread, cheese and cold cuts.

Her eyes were on him when he walked back in. Eirik wondered what warranted such close scrutiny.

"I hope this is to your liking. If not, there's always room service. They're sure to have whatever you desire."

"This is great, really." Elle curled her elegant hands around her mug and took a sip. Two more and color began to seep into her cheeks. That was something at least.

They ate in companionable silence for a few minutes before she uttered the words that nearly had him choking on his food.

"I'm going to help you but you've got to do something for me, too." She caught his gaze and held it. "I want you to teach me how to drive a man crazy."

Chapter Four

Lust slammed into Eirik. Did she know what she was saying? He stared at Elle for a long, hazy second. The things he could show her. The things he *wanted* to show her.

He clamped down on the urge to grab her and drag her into the bedroom to do just that. Eirik needed to know that it *was* what she was asking and not wishful thinking on his part.

Putting down his coffee with more care than was necessary, Eirik cleared his throat. It was so tight it was a struggle to form the word, "Explain."

Elle bit her bottom lip as if she was second guessing her words. Letting her back out now wasn't an option.

"I just need to know I heard you correctly. That this is what you really want." He touched her then. Unable to stop himself from gliding a hand up her arm. Feeling that silky skin.

A prelude? He hoped so.

"I'm guessing that you know your way around a woman and have been with enough of us to know what works when it comes to seduction." She shyly met his gaze. "On both sides of the table."

He didn't want to scare her off, so he merely shrugged. If she was trying to get him to admit to just how many women he'd been with, she wasn't going to receive an answer. Even though the number wasn't astronomical the way the tabloids or his parents thought, Eirik liked to consider himself a gentleman. At least to some extent. Also, Eirik wanted her to continue before she lost her nerve. Diving into that conversation would do nothing to help that.

So he waited for her to continue with patience he never knew he possessed.

She gazed at him, her eyes luminous. "I want to learn how to win Greg back."

Shock drove him back in his seat. That was the absolute last thing that he wanted to hear. After everything they'd talked about, that was her conclusion? That was what she wanted?

"You want to win that ass back?"

Elle gave him a look that glittered with contempt. "If you'd let me finish. I want to get him back so that I can crush him. But I want him to see me the way he sees Celina. A goddess that he would be lucky to share air with."

That she thought of herself to be less than Celina rankled Eirik. In the little time they'd spent together, he already knew that Elle's little toe was worth far more than a thousand Celinas.

"So what's my role in all this?" He slid a solitary finger up her arm. Leaned in closer. "Simply as a tutor? Do you want me to put together some PowerPoint presentations or something?"

She swallowed before taking a slow breath then lifted her burning gaze to meet his.

Licking her lips, she said, "I'm a hands-on learner, so I was hoping you'd be open to a more practical role."

That was all Eirik needed to hear.

Picking her up was easy — small and fine-boned, Elle weighed next to nothing. Eirik wound her legs around his hips, delved his hands into her hair and kissed her in one smooth series of moves. As if it was something they did all the time, they lined up perfectly and sank into the kiss.

She tasted like heaven.

Elle clung to him and let out a mewling sound that only made him harder. Had him gripping her closer.

Winding an arm around her and curling a hand under Elle to support her weight gave him the chance to feel the soft curve of her bottom and left him free to slip his other hand under her T-shirt and bra. He pushed her lingerie up and out of the way so there was no impediment to his exploration.

Then, at last, he did what he had been aching to do all day and cupped her breast to brush his thumb over her beaded nipple.

Elle arched into his touch, gasping into his mouth while he gently squeezed and caressed.

Though he would have loved to continue kissing her, there were other parts of her that he needed to taste.

Eirik kept walking until she was pressed against a wall. He hitched her up higher then held her in place with his torso so that both hands were free to yank the shirt off, followed in quick succession by her bra. He tossed them aside and gazed at her, lust darkening his eyes.

"Beautiful."

It had been Angie's voice at the back of her mind telling her to move on, laced with the crazy need for Eirik which had prompted her to make the ludicrous request. It was an asinine idea, but it was a plan at least. She'd get revenge and the man in front of her all in one go. *How's that for taking life into my own hands?*

Though now, with Eirik staring in a way that had her almost believing she was the most beautiful thing he'd ever seen, reasons were moot. Incredulity was the last thing that crossed her mind before he closed his lips around the peak of her breast and sucked her into his hot mouth.

She tangled her fingers in his hair and held him tightly, not wanting the sensations to ever end.

The rasp of his beard on her delicate skin stoked the fire in her even higher. How could she have ever thought facial hair was a turn-off? Eirik's hair abrading her skin was the most erotic thing she'd ever experienced. Just his tongue brushing her hard nipple wound her tighter.

And he had barely even begun to touch her.

Goosebumps formed, blooming from where his lips met her and spread over her sensitized skin. She wanted to know what it felt like when he touched her everywhere. Anywhere. Elle wanted Eirik to explore and caress anything. *Everything.*

By the time he moved to her other aching breast, Elle trembled from head to toe and was oh so close to an orgasm that she was sure the slightest breeze would send her over.

As if sensing just how close she was, Eirik gave her a final lick before leaning back to admire her once again. He said nothing as he held her gaze.

No, Eirik peering into her soul with his honey-colored eyes was the most erotic thing she'd ever experienced. He studied her. Delved into her heart, her mind, her very being with those incredible eyes.

He reached up and cupped her cheeks before capturing her lips again.

Elle needed to feel his skin against hers. It took her a few tries to get her trembling hands to grip his shirt and pull it upward. Eirik only broke contact long enough to tug the shirt off and throw it aside. The movement loosened his hair. It fell to his shoulders, wafting his scent with it. There was a slight tang of musk from his run, but that tantalizing smell of him had her mouth-watering.

She tangled her fingers in his hair while she grazed her chest against his. The sparse dusting of hair on his had very much the same effect on her as his beard had and more. Elle pressed herself close against his hard form.

Elle let her hands wander over him, exploring the hard expanse of muscle and hot skin.

Eirik continued to plunder her mouth as though she was the very air he needed. That his life depended on finding every secret place in her mouth. On her body.

His roving hands sought out and caressed every part of her that had been revealed, tracing her skin. Learning what made her sigh. What made her gasp. What had her mewling and moaning.

What left her wet and aching.

What made her beg him for more.

And he knew exactly what he was doing. Eirik caressed, licked, bit, point after point and each one turning her further into a quivering bundle of nerves and need.

What confounded her was that all this was done without wandering below the waist. With nothing more than kisses and caresses. Without trying. What could Eirik do if he applied himself?

Elle got the impression she'd be ruined for anyone else, but she was quite willing to find out.

Head back against the wall and eyes closed, Elle was more than ready to give up control to him. Eirik had free rein to do whatever he liked if he kept her feeling this way.

He wrapped his arms around her to hold her secure and started walking. Elle knew he was taking them somewhere, but she was too busy kissing him back to take any real notice. After what seemed like seconds later, she could swear she heard a door being kicked shut before she was lowered to stand on the floor.

It was then that she noticed just how different in height they were. At a stretch, she was just tall enough to peek over his shoulder. Meanwhile, Eirik filled the room with his presence, which only made her feel smaller. More feminine. Shirtless, with his hair loose and his eyes burning, he looked like a marauding Viking ready to stake his claim. Elle sensed the wildness in him. But rather than quail from it, she was entranced.

Elle wanted him. Needed him. Didn't care how she got him.

Licking her bottom lip, she reached for Eirik, pressed her palms flat against his chest. So solid and burning under her touch. On impulse, she leaned in and flicked her tongue over his nipple. And again, taking pleasure in the way his breath hitched. Though every muscle in his body tensed, he didn't touch her.

Elle did the same to his other nipple, touching it with the tip of her tongue at first before licking with a bolder stroke. The move drew a growling breath from Eirik. She trailed her fingers lower, bumping over his abs to come to the low-slung waistband of his shorts.

Not sure she was brave enough to deal with that quite yet, Elle traced the barrier, following it to his chiseled sides and back. Was there any inch of this man that wasn't solid muscle?

As she glided her hands back to the drawstring under his belly button, her hand came into contact with the head of his erection that strained to push through the soft fabric.

Jerking as if it has burned her, Elle bit her lip. She'd come this far. Grazing the head with her fingers, she didn't stop the little smile that curved her lips when he hissed. Heat blasted through her with the realization that she had the power to do this to him. That she could bring him pleasure.

Elle dragged her fingers down the ridge, intrigued by the length and girth her fingers encountered. Like the rest of him, his cock was big and hard. Intimidating.

The urge to see all of him overrode any residual reticence.

The instant she tugged the drawstring knot loose, Eirik gripped her hands.

Elle tipped her head back to look at him.

Eirik's jaw was clenched, his entire body thrummed with tension. "Are you sure about this?"

She had started nodding before he got half way through the sentence. She needed him. *Now.* "Absolutely."

Something that sounded like a cross between arousal and relief rumbled through him when he picked her up and laid her on the bed.

His gaze raked over her skin with almost tangible heat for a second before he pushed the shorts down over his hips and let them drop to the floor.

Perfectly at ease with his nudity, he stood over her, giving her time to look her fill.

For a moment, Elle fought to breathe. And why wouldn't he be comfortable? Eirik was absolutely beautiful. He could have easily been carved from stone by a master artist. His proportions were perfect. His muscles sculpted. And the evidence of his gender very impressive.

Elle licked her lips, earning a groan from her Viking.

"When you do that..." Eirik muttered something guttural. He grabbed her by the ankles and dragged her to the edge of the bed. Kneeling on the floor next to the bed, he still reached her with little exertion. Not giving her a chance to think, he hooked her legs over his shoulders. With a wicked smile, he lowered his head between her thighs.

Elle's mind scrambled even more at the feel of his beard scraping the delicate skin of her inner thighs. All further thought was obliterated when he closed his mouth on her wet slit.

"Eirik..." The ability to form words or even coherent images fled when he ran his tongue over her aching flesh. Sparks flashed behind her eyelids as she arched under him, totally at his mercy.

He laved her with sure strokes of his tongue, winding up her pleasure until it burst.

Clawing her hands in his hair, she gripped him to her, her cries echoing in the room. Her orgasm concentrated into a ball of white-hot fire low in her belly before exploding. The sheer power of it ripped through her. Her reaction seemed to spur him on to use his mouth and tongue on her to devastate her further.

All the strength ebbed out of her, leaving Elle panting but unable to move her limbs. Being so languid was something she'd never experienced before. At least not after sex with Greg. It was nice but never earth-shattering.

Then it hit her. They hadn't had sex yet.

Elle opened her eyes to find him lying on his side next to her, observing her with a gentle expression on his face.

"Are you okay?"

Nodding, she managed a shy smile. "I feel amazing."

The look on his face morphed into a proud smirk. "Good."

Because she could feel he was building up to something, Elle simply stared up at him.

"Think you're up to the final part of the lesson then?"

Lesson? It took her a full second to remember what he was talking about. Had she, in actuality, asked him to teach her how to seduce a man?

She nodded. "I am."

"I don't think that you need to be taught a thing, by the way." He shifted so she felt the press of his erection against her thigh. "As you can tell, I find you very arousing."

For now. What about when the novelty wore off? It didn't matter at the moment. The sensation of him pressed so intimately against her had Elle focusing on the here and now. And right now she needed Eirik.

Not quite believing her own audacity, Elle reached for him. "Show me how much."

Eirik was torn between spreading her under him to plunge his throbbing body into her and taking his time to explore to his heart's content.

How is it possible Elle thinks she needs to learn how to seduce someone? He hadn't known her a day and he was in a constant state of arousal. And how easy had it been to get him into bed? She'd all but snapped her fingers.

Unsure of what to take from that but knowing he didn't like how easily she had wrapped him around her little finger, Eirik needed to show her who was boss.

Sliding her up the bed, he studied her. Elle's chest and cheeks were still stained pink with arousal and her eyes heavy. Her sweet lips were swollen from her biting them. Her scent was still in the air and her taste on his lips. But he wanted more. If he wasn't careful, he'd leave himself wide open to Elle and she would be able to worm her way under his skin with ease.

He would just have to make sure that he got her out of his system first.

This was about pleasure and revenge. Pleasure being his most immediate concern.

Eirik lowered his head to brush his lips against hers.

Elle was so petite but her figure perfect. All he could see and feel of her body was, to his delight, flawless. Her skin smooth and without a blemish, and Eirik had had every opportunity to spot any.

Running a hand up her side, he noted how her skin roughened with goosebumps at his touch. How she arched into his hand like a kitten. Hell, she more or less purred at his touch.

And it's all for me.

What would she do once he was inside her?

His body clenched with anticipation.

Smug that she responded so well to him, he continued the slow trek up her torso to cup her breast. With his other hand, Eirik toyed with the ends of her hair.

She was so willing to let him do whatever he liked. Eirik knew that would stay the same as long as she was being pleasured. He would make sure that, for however long this lasted, she would be putty in his hands.

Elle was right in assuming that he'd had plenty of lovers. Since discovering the delights of the female body when he was seventeen years old, he hadn't found himself without a willing body in his bed whenever he wanted.

He knew what Elle wanted and he was more than willing to give it to her.

Cock in hand, he surged over her, ready to notch the head of it inside her. Eirik licked his lips at the delicious sensation of contact. Skin to skin. At long last.

Wait. A tiny voice in the back of his mind broke through the haze.

He hadn't brought any protection with him. Groaning, Eirik lurched back. "Elle, tell me you have a condom."

Dazed she gazed up at him and for a moment he wasn't sure if she'd even heard what he'd asked. But as her eyes cleared, she slowly shook her head. "No."

He tried to pull away. But she clung to him. "Elle…" he groaned. Eirik shook with the effort it took him to hold back. "I'm trying to do the right thing."

"I'm on the pill."

He kissed her again only to break it moments later to meet her gaze. "Are you sure about this?"

Elle responded by wrapping a leg around his hip. Eirik was delighted by her passionate determination. She tugged him down so that their bodies aligned. "I am."

Heat blasted through Eirik at her vehemence. At how much she wanted him. Not that his knees weren't shaking at the thought of being inside her. *Bare.*

The prospect of doing something he'd never done with anyone let alone someone so alluring added to the slight tremor he'd been fighting. Now wasn't the time to act like an untried youth. Eirik would prove to her that she'd come to the right person to teach her about sex.

Kissing her, Eirik followed a path down her neck. Elle's sigh and moan of pleasure sent more blood surging into his cock, hardening him to the point of pain. He needed to be inside her now.

Nipping the silky skin of her throat, he took himself in hand and swiped the head of his erection over her wet folds. The sensation as he pushed into her was exquisite. Eirik bit his lip, struggling to keep from slamming into her and feeling her slick, tight heat gripped around him.

Somehow, he found the strength and presence of mind to push his aching cock into her slowly. Gently.

He lifted his head, wanting to see her expression, and found her staring at him with wide, glazed eyes as if the pleasure she was experiencing was beyond belief.

Eirik grinned at her. She had no idea.

He thrust to the hilt, pushing the last few inches of himself into her — going as deep as he was able — groaning when she clenched around him in reaction. She was so snug, so wet and hot that Eirik struggled not to give into his body's urges or this would be over too soon.

Elle was so small he had to give her a chance to get used to his body. No matter how badly he wanted to pound into her again and again.

Eyes closed, he dropped his head to her shoulder as he waited out the need to come. To move. To drive himself so far inside her that he would be embedded.

An eternity later, Elle's hands cupped his cheeks and lifted his head to look at her. Running her tongue over his tightly closed mouth, she tentatively lifted her hips, shifting him inside her.

Groaning, he hitched his cock deep, then pulled as far out of her as he could bring himself to before plunging back into her.

"Eirik...you feel...amazing."

So did she. Incredible. Without question. "You haven't felt anything yet."

Elle had never experienced anything like Eirik's possession. The words had barely left his lips before he closed his hands on her thighs and tugged her into his stroke, maximizing the sensation with each plunge into her body.

When he had first pushed his massive cock into her, Elle had been sure that she was going to be split in two. But the deeper he got, the more of him she took into herself, the more the pleasure intensified.

Then he'd started to move.

Elle clung to him, loving what he did — what he was doing — to her. Giving up control to Eirik had been strangely liberating. To allow someone she had only met control over any part of her life, let alone letting them have full run of her body, was something she would never have done before. Then again Greg had hardly inspired this kind of abandon and they'd been together for years.

The delicious sparks of sensation crackled through her with every surge of his hips, igniting what felt like every single one of her nerve endings. The feel of him so big and hard against her — inside her — was, for lack of a better description, divine.

It didn't take long for him to bring her to the edge again, but Elle hung on, wanting to go over the precipice with him. At the same time. It was stupid, but it was what she wanted. What she needed more than anything right in that moment.

"Look at me, Elle."

The husky entreaty drew her gaze to meet his and she found herself drawn into their honeyed depths. Unable to look away, everything was amplified. His body was harder, the pleasure insurmountable. Elle felt every inch of skin that touched, every brush of hair against her, from chest to thighs, to groin.

Then he grew bigger — harder — inside her. *Is that possible?*

"Come for me, Elle. Come with me," he groaned.

It was another two deep strokes of his magnificent cock before Elle's world exploded. Still captured by his gaze, she saw the moment he lost control. Though his eyes glazed over slightly, he was still with her. He saw her as they came apart. That just made her own orgasm — their connection — that much stronger.

Gripping her hips tight, Eirik pushed into her with almost savage determination to get closer. Deeper.

Elle wrapped herself around him, not wanting the moment to end. She felt every pulse of his cock. Every spasm of sensation coursing through him.

It was while she was afloat in a sea of bliss that she reminded herself that this wasn't love. This was just physical. An arrangement. She was getting back at Greg. Moving on with her life. Doing what she wanted for once.

She had to keep things in perspective.

Wriggling under him, Elle knew there was little hope of being able to shift him without his cooperation.

Eirik rolled, dragging her with him until she lay half-sprawled over him.

It felt so good. Why did everything about Eirik feel so wonderful?

Elle gave up trying to analyze things and drifted off to sleep, secure in his arms.

Chapter Five

Elle woke up disorientated but wonderfully loose and relaxed. *Happy.* It was something she hadn't truly felt in a long time.

And so wrong.

She had just been dumped by her long-time boyfriend and here she was…blissful. And in the arms of another man.

She let her gaze wander over the man still asleep and tangled in the sheets next to her. In repose, Eirik was just as beautiful, but less intimidating. Taking the chance to get a good look at him without similar scrutiny, Elle smiled.

He was achingly gorgeous. And with his hair loose and wild, he truly looked like the Viking she had imagined him to be when they'd first met. What would he look like without the beard and the hair? It didn't take too much work to deduce that he would still be handsome enough to turn her knees to jelly without either.

They'd spent the night wound around each other and she had twice woken up with him kissing her, which had led to him flipping her over and teaching her that there was more than one way to blow her mind. She had been the instigator of the third and, with his help, she learned to ride him like a champion. Elle wasn't sure who started on who the fourth time, only that it had left them both replete and entangled so that neither wanted to move — and hadn't — until now.

It still seemed magical to her that in the few hours they'd been in bed they'd managed bone-melting sex four times. Her experiences in the past had paled in comparison. Each time with Eirik had been more incredible than the last. His stamina and skill were incredible.

Even now she was tempted to climb on top of him again and wake him up to explore each other's bodies once more, but she had to get her head on straight and figure out a plan. Having sex with Eirik again wasn't going to help her straighten out anything, let alone her thoughts.

As she stared at him, lost in thought, he curled his hand around her waist and tugged her closer in one swift move.

Squealing, in equal parts startled and delighted, Elle laughed. Pushing back against his shoulders, she angled her head in for the kiss he seemed to be after.

He brushed his lips against hers before he opened her eyes. On a contented sigh, he said, "Good morning."

"Morning." Elle knew she should get out of bed and start the day, but she just didn't have the strength to make herself move from the wonderful cocoon of masculinity wrapped around her.

She felt too good. And it had everything to do with Eirik.

"Sleep well?"

When she had slept, it had been great. And when she hadn't, it had been even better. Elle nodded.

He checked his phone for the time and sighed. "I suppose we should get up." Though it sounded like the last thing he wanted to do.

He ran his hand over her side, down her thigh then back up to toy with her hair as if he was reminding himself of the night before and giving himself reasons not to start the day.

To be honest, it would take something earth shattering to convince her to leave the bed right then.

In the end, it was Eirik who made the first reluctant move.

Elle watched him stand, naked and magnificent, next to the bed. Seeing him by the light of day, completely bare and unselfconscious of his nudity, brought home the night before with startling clarity.

But seeing him fully illuminated for the first time was a delight that knocked the breath from her lungs and sent heat coursing to her other parts.

His eyes burned as he swept his gaze over her. "If you keep looking at me like that, we're not going to get out of here for a very long time."

Would that really be so bad?

As if divining her thoughts, Eirik gave her a mock scowl that morphed turned into a handsome grin when he fell back onto the bed.

Laughing, she fought him with playful shoves at his shoulders when he half landed on her. As if she stood a chance against someone of his size. She screeched with delight as he tickled her into submission and wrestled her under him. Breathless and fizzing with happiness, Elle smiled up at him before nuzzling her nose into his beard.

He tangled his legs with hers, with laughter rumbling through him. Elle rubbed hers up and down them, enjoying the roughness. She reveled in the differences between their bodies. Eirik was hard where she was soft. Large to her petite. They complemented each other well. And not just because they were so compatible sexually.

Heat flared at the memories of the night before that flooded into her mind.

Elle arched against his upper body, loving the sensation of his hair against the sensitive skin of her breasts.

Eirik moaned as he ground his hardening erection against her. After one night together, she knew how to push his buttons, just like he knew exactly how to push hers.

With her hands into his hair, she tangled her fingers in the smooth tendrils while he slowly rubbed his body against hers. Eirik ran his hands over her as if he was memorizing the feel of her.

Lust rushed through Elle's veins, adding to the happiness already pinging though her. *How glorious would it be to wake up to this every morning?*

It would be divine. Elle was already becoming addicted to the man over her.

His warm eyes met hers and, for that instant, she could see the future with him. Eirik's soft, dreamy gaze had her almost believing he pictured the same thing.

Then, as though he'd flipped a switch, his eyes turned hard. Angry.

No.

Elle pulled back from him the same moment he jerked back.

As he lurched from the bed, it was as if a wall had been erected between them. He turned into a cold Viking. Fearsome and icy.

Tugging the sheet up higher, Elle watched him grab his clothes and stalked from the room.

What had just happened?

Elle stumbled off the bed. Dragging the sheet with her, she made the shortest walk of shame imaginable into the en suite bathroom and kicked the door shut.

Eirik swiped his hair out of his face and glared at himself in the mirror of his bathroom. What the hell was he thinking? This wasn't a romantic vacation. This was business. He had to keep that in mind.

So what if sex with Elle had been incredible? There was more at stake here than a great time in bed. Though the bed was only one of the many places he pictured him and Elle.

That was a problem.

He had never imagined how addictive she would be. How responsive to him. The hope had been to get her out of his system last night and prove that he'd been the right one for her to come to with her request. The need for her had only seemed to burn hotter the second, third and fourth time they'd come together. Then to wake up and want her again with the same intensity? It was unprecedented.

Unsettling.

Eirik's body tightened again from him just thinking about her under him, flushed and gasping. He had to dig deep to keep from returning to the room and throwing her back on the bed to spend the rest of their time together exploring the blistering chemistry that burned between them.

Definitely an impulse he had to stanch if he was going to get anywhere with his revenge plan.

Keeping focus with Elle around was a challenge. But not something that would compromise him.

He wouldn't let it.

He was there for a reason.

Eirik focused on the anger, the shame, of having been used and tossed aside by Celina. On what she'd attempted to do to him and his family. What she and Elle's ex had both tried.

That was what he needed to keep sight of.

The sound of Elle slamming something caught his attention.

He had gotten a glimpse of her face when he'd turned to walk out and her expression had cut deep. He'd hurt Elle as if he'd reached out and slapped her in the face. She didn't deserve that. Not after everything that she had just gone through the past few days. The last thing Elle needed was him treating her so horribly when she'd done nothing to deserve it.

What they needed was to have some clear-cut rules that they had to adhere to.

He turned on the shower hard and cold. What he needed to do was think. Which wasn't possible with a raging erection or with the cause of it so close.

Stepping under the chilly stream rid him of one problem, but the images of Elle under him, loving everything he did and all but begging for more, were a lot harder to erase. Did he really want them gone?

Aside from it having been the most satisfying night of his life, Eirik had felt a connection with Elle that he didn't with anyone else.

He pushed the notion away.

Ridiculous. It was just good sex. Really good sex. That he wanted more of…

When twenty minutes of ice-cold water didn't help cool his ardor, Eirik gave up. Would anything help until he'd worked her out of his system?

He'd had great bed partners in the past, but he had learned early on that compatibility in bed didn't mean anything in the long run. In the end he'd get bored or she would become tiresome and they would move on. *Just like it will this time.*

After getting dressed at a more rapid pace than usual, Eirik exited. Elle was nowhere to be seen. *Has she left?*

Heart beating a little faster at the thought, he found himself skirting past her room. The sounds coming from the other side reassured him that she hadn't run.

Because she was essential to his revenge plot. That was all.

What plot? His body throbbed as if to call him a liar.

Ignoring the instinct to barge into her room, Eirik knocked on the door. "Elle? Was there anything you wanted for breakfast?"

"I'm fine," came her quiet reply.

She didn't sound fine. "Are you coming out?"

Elle muttered something incoherent. Unsettled by the strange sensation burning in his gut, Eirik retreated to the living area. He went straight to the tablet embedded in the wall and ordered breakfast.

Why he chose that one, he had no idea.

Lies. He knew exactly what he was doing. There were tablets that were strategically dotted around the place. He could have even called it in, the way he had the night before. But no. He chose to hover close to listen to her.

Not that it mattered. Now that the meal had been ordered, he was left with nothing to do but wait.

Something he absolutely hated doing.

Patience wasn't Eirik's strong suit. Never had been. There was nothing in his power to do that would hurry either Elle or the meal along, however.

Plotting, at least, was something he could do. With Elle here in the villa with him, there were all manner of scenarios they would be able to enact to irk the couple next door.

His favorite scenario thus far had been to take Elle's plan of making her ex want her again and push it a step further. He'd make Celina beg to be with him. He would give in, after a time of course, then watch as she dumped her new lover. Then when she thought all was well, he'd present her with the proof of her crimes before watching her get escorted away by the authorities. Of course, it was preferable that the final stage happened in front of a large audience so everyone knew what kind of woman she was. Then Henning would go crawling back to Elle where she would do the same.

Celina would be easy to entice and it would only be a matter of time before she came running back to him. But it didn't feel like it was enough. He wanted to destroy her for the way she had tried to ruin him. But was it even possible?

The woman didn't have any scruples or anyone she cared about. Not truly. There was no family that he knew of. Not that it mattered since all the woman worried about was herself.

Why the hell had he gotten with her? He'd known from the off she was bad news. He'd been told she was a nasty piece of work. Yet he'd let himself get drawn into her web of seduction. He knew she'd been playing him, maybe not from the beginning but early on, and yet he hadn't cared and had carried on until it blew up in his face. And the sex had been nothing compared to what he'd experienced with Elle the previous night. It was as if he had been looking for a way to self-destruct.

He wasn't going to let himself get taken again. No amount of sex was going to cloud his judgement. No matter how stellar.

Or addictive.

Glowering, Eirik stalked to the balcony to brood.

Elle took a deep breath and opened the door to her bedroom. A quick peek didn't reveal Eirik, though she knew he had been lurking there not too long before.

What was she so scared of anyway? Facing Eirik? What had happened the night before was nothing to be ashamed of. They were two consenting adults. And it had been good. Incredibly so.

Then why the unease now?

Because he'd jumped out of bed and walked out on her just as they were about to re-enact the night before didn't mean she'd done anything wrong. In fact, from his reactions during the night and this morning, she'd done everything right. And they'd both wanted more. At least up until he'd shut down on her, leaving her and obliterating any feelings of empowerment and enjoyment she had gained.

Stomach churning, Elle knew what she wanted to do. The desire to get back to her villa and put some space between them was a strong one. Though that idea appealed to her, Elle wouldn't let herself run. Not this time.

Being meek and retiring was what had got her there in the first place. Had she been stronger, Greg wouldn't have left her. In fact, she might not have gotten with him at all. Elle refused to let herself get used again.

By any man. In any manner.

Eirik thought he could just tumble her into bed then forget about her until she became useful to his plan? He had another think coming.

By the time Elle reached the living room, she was spoiling for a fight. Only, it was empty. Where was he? Had he left the villa altogether?

Not sure what to make of that, Elle wandered toward the kitchen. As she did, she went over the events of the night before.

One moment she'd been depressed and crying out on deck and the next…

Dammit! *My phone!*

Elle remembered in vivid detail having launched her phone off the deck into the darkness. Another burst of anger and frustration that had been so out of character for her.

Then again, why not let her emotions loose when this whole trip had started because she was behaving unlike she usually would?

Fiancé leaves? Why not chase him? Meet some man on the beach who invites me back for dinner at his villa? Sure, go! Then why not sleep with him, too! Multiple times!

Running her hands through her hair, Elle let hysterical laughter bubble up her throat to accompany the strange disassociation she felt with herself. As if she was outside of her body, watching herself heading toward a colossal train wreck.

This is what a breakdown must feel like.

Still giggling, Elle walked out to the deck. Maybe she'd spot her phone and find out if it was salvageable.

She returned to where she had been sitting then peered over the railing. Would she even be able to find it? Knowing her luck, someone had probably found it and taken it. If it was still in one piece, that was.

How hard had she thrown it?

She peered down at the dark rocks below. There was no chance of it having survived if it had hit them or if it had landed in the water, but if it had landed on the sand…

Elle stretched out to search the white sand for a dash of black. It wasn't long before she reached out so far she was precariously balanced with her hips on the railing. On a whim, she kicked her legs up behind her, not caring how she might appear to onlookers. It was fun. And when was the last time she had fun just for fun's sake?

The enjoyment didn't last long when a familiar voice shouted, "Are you trying to hurt yourself?"

On a sigh, Elle dropped back onto the deck then turned to find Eirik jogging toward her. Today he wore an entirely different pair of faded blue jeans. She only knew they were a new pair because the rips were in different places. His choice of shirt this time was a white linen button-down, however. Eirik had tied his hair up again but rather than a bun, it was back in a half ponytail.

And, as always, he looked good.

Elle didn't want to be admiring him but couldn't seem to help herself. It only angered her more.

"What does it matter to you?" Elle knew she sounded like a recalcitrant child but it was too late to do anything about it now.

"What were you doing?" He reached a hand out to her but almost immediately dropped it to his side.

Biting back a sigh, hurt that he hadn't touched her and angry at herself for even caring, she snarled, "I was looking for my phone, if you must know."

"This one?" He held out the battered phone.

"How did you find it?" Elle carefully took the shards of glass and mangled metal from him, not needing a second glance to know that it was beyond repair.

"It was thrown at my head last night when I was on my way back from my jog."

"Did it hit you?"

He scoffed and shook his head. "No. I managed to deflect it."

Elle scowled at the remnants of her phone. Was it bad that she almost wished that it had hit him?

"Had I known it was your phone, I would have tried to catch it."

She shrugged. "Doesn't matter now."

"I'll replace it," he offered, his voice soft.

"That isn't necessary." As if she needed to be in debt to him for anything.

He frowned. "Of course it is. You can't be without a phone."

"I'm sure I'll survive." She glanced at her splintered reflection in the shattered screen.

"There must people you need to keep in contact with."

No one outside of Angie, really. Not wanting to share how decrepit and small her circle of friends was, Elle just shrugged. "I don't plan on being away that much longer."

Eirik glowered. "I thought we had an understanding."

"What if I've changed my mind?"

His expression darkened. "If this is because of last night—"

"No, it's because of this morning." Elle pulled herself up to her full height—not that it made much difference when facing down a man with Eirik's build. "I thought last night was...was..."

"Incredible?"

The way he said it dropped her stomach. So calm. So plain. So, it had been just another roll in the hay for him. Heat climbed into her cheeks. "A one-time thing."

Eirik cupped her cheek. "I seriously hope you're kidding about that, because last night was amazing. *You* were—are—amazing."

His words stunned her. For several long breaths all she could do was stare at him. Eirik looked completely sincere. "But then why did you—"

"Because it's never been like that for me." He kept her from turning away. "I mean that."

Elle didn't know how to quantify the soaring emotions whirling through her at his words. Even the nagging doubt that they were true didn't stop the delight from pinging through her system.

Needing her head clear, she stepped out of his embrace. "So then why did you leave like that?"

"My emotions were—" Eirik followed her, keeping close enough that she sensed the heat coming off him. "I handled it badly. I'm sorry."

He seemed sincere enough, but then she had thought she and Greg were solid up until a few days ago. Didn't that just prove that she wasn't the best judge of character? Now, in particular, when she was so out of her head that she'd chased Greg around the planet only to then sleep with another man?

A man that stood before her, tempting her to drag him right back into bed?

Hadn't Eirik made it very clear that he was there to get revenge on his girlfriend and had got it into his head that she was a useful tool in his quest? It was conceivable that this was a ruse just to get her to stay.

Elle caught movement out of the corner of her eye and turned to see Greg and Celina entangled on their patio, driving a spike further through her self-confidence.

Eirik followed her gaze and reacted by wrapping an arm around her shoulder and steering her back into the villa. "Let's go inside."

She held her ground. "Let's have breakfast outside."

A little smirk of admiration curled the corner of her mouth before he redirected her to the table. "It's a lovely morning for it." Eirik brushed his lips against her. Then, as if out of habit, he pulled out a chair for her. He observed her with a secretive little smile while she made herself comfortable. "I'll be right back."

Nodding, she settled into her seat. Eirik had given her a chair with a perfect view across the way. Not wanting to be seen watching the other couple, she angled herself away so that they were in her peripheral view.

Even from a distance, she observed Greg peeking over Celina's shoulder to stare in her direction. Was it just by chance? It turned out that it wasn't when Elle caught him doing it at regular intervals.

Snickering under her breath, Elle allowed herself a deep inhalation of the salty sea air. He wouldn't get a rise out of her.

"What's so amusing?"

Eirik had walked out with a couple of coffees and a tray. He placed one cup in front of Elle before taking the seat next to her.

"Them." She tilted her head, indicating the villa across the stretch of beach.

If she didn't know better, she never would have imagined he even knew the couple next door. They held none of his interest and he didn't even bother glancing in their direction.

What surprised her was, as if it was something they did every day, he reached down and lifted her legs so that her feet ended up in his lap. He massaged one while he sipped his coffee.

They took a leisured breakfast. Eirik had ordered an assortment of succulent fruit and buttery croissants to enjoy with their drinks. Exactly what she would have ordered. The mix of sweet and bitter hit the spot that morning.

This was something that she might well get used to — with ease — but shouldn't even entertain the thought of. Even if what he said about his impression of the night before was true, this wasn't the start of a relationship. At least, not a stable and sustainable one.

Once the lust and initial excitement wore off what would be left? Nothing.

And she'd be back right where she was after Greg's abandonment.

But hadn't that landed her in Eirik's arms?

She was just going around in pointless circles. The fact of the matter was, she needed to make a change in her life. Elle had known that for a while, but she'd always assumed that Greg would be a part of those changes.

So, because of him, she was going to make a bunch of stupid mistakes to make a point? *No.* This was about exploring who she was now. A woman free to make her own choices and follow her head and heart wherever they took her. If she chose to follow.

Sleeping with Eirik might not have been the smartest thing she could do, but it had felt amazing and taught her a few things about herself, her body, what this man was like. This was about getting life experience. Seeing and doing things she never had or even imagined.

"You're pensive this morning."

Elle lifted her gaze to meet his. As if Eirik knew what she was like on a typical one. "Just enjoying the peace and quiet."

Eirik nodded. "Are your mornings usually hectic?"

Now that she thought about it, not for the past few years. At least not how he more than likely pictured it. She had cleared pretty much everything out of her life to make Greg a priority. Her mornings started two hours before he woke to fit in some yoga. Then she'd get his breakfast and make sure his clothes were ready. Once he was out of the door, she was left cleaning and organizing an already immaculate apartment until it was time to make dinner and await his return.

What an idiot she'd been.

Shaking her head, she hoped that Eirik would take the cue and embrace the tranquility of the moment, too.

He did. And resumed rubbing her foot, too.

As far as moments went, Elle considered this a perfect one. Minus the circumstances of their being there together, of course. Taking another sip of her coffee, Elle let her eyes drift closed while she listened to the cadence of her heart, her breath, the sea, the melodies of them all coming together in glorious harmony in her mind.

The exhilaration of music flowing so freely in her head was short-lived. Why didn't she have anything to write with when inspiration struck her?

"What's wrong?"

"Nothing." Irritated that he'd interrupted her train of thought, she glared at him. What was he doing? Studying her every move and expression?

"Something is bothering you. I can see it."

Either her skill at hiding her feelings wasn't what she'd thought it was or he had to be the most perceptive man ever. Or it might have been that she wasn't used to being with someone who paid so much attention to her feelings. "Maybe it's the man who keeps interrupting my quiet time."

He pressed his lips together looking slightly peeved. "Try another."

"There's nothing you can do about it, so what does it matter?"

"Of course it matters." He patted her leg. "And unless you tell me, you'll never know if I can help or not."

Sighing, Elle rolled her eyes at him. "You really are overbearing, you know that?" Even as she said it, she knew it was just her irritation talking. Eirik was being kind, if annoying and persistent. Elle met his gaze. "If you must know, I had an idea but no way of writing it down."

He shifted at once to stand. "There's some stationery inside. I can get it for you now…"

Shaking her head, Elle dragged her feet off his lap. "It's not that kind of idea. Paper isn't what I need. At least, not that kind of paper."

Eirik gave her a puzzled smile. "Do enlighten me."

"I've been thinking about writing music again."

"You write music?"

"I used to." Not wanting to look him in the eyes, she turned her attention to the water. "I haven't in years because the inspiration just wasn't there. But being here..."

"Has rekindled the spark? I get it."

Did he? Elle learned at an early age that creative minds and non-creative minds worked in very different ways. Her parents had seemed baffled by how her train of thought functioned. Or rather, how she'd lose herself in the music coming together inside her head to the point where she would lose large chunks of time. Greg certainly hadn't understood it, not that he'd tried. What were the chances that Eirik did or even was able?

Giving him a small smile, Elle changed the subject. "Last night isn't something I do."

Eirik smirked. "I think what you did last night was something you do very well."

Heat flooded her body at the recollection of just *what* she had done. What *he* had done. "That's not what I meant and you know it." Wishing rubbing the blush from her cheeks was an ability she would spontaneously manifest, Elle leveled her gaze at him. "Jumping into a bed with a man I barely know...it's not me."

He nodded and digested that information. "So you regret last night?"

Did she? Was it weird that she didn't? It had been an amazing experience. One that had opened her eyes to what good sex was.

And just how out of her mind she was thanks to everything that was going on.

She shook her head. "A little embarrassed, maybe."

Eirik closed a hand over her knee. "You have nothing to be ashamed of. You're a grown woman who made the choice to sleep with a man. Simple as that."

"It's just...I've never...lost control like that."

"You want to know a secret?"

Elle met his gaze and nodded.

"Me neither."

Chapter Six

Eirik wasn't sure what had prompted him to tell her that. What he did know, however, was that she relaxed at his admission. As if at least one of the barriers she had erected against him had come down.

It wouldn't take too much work to convince her to join him on an excursion around the resort.

He waited until most of the food had been eaten before asking, "Why don't we do a little exploring today? We can stretch our legs and see what this place has to offer."

Elle pursed her lips. "While letting people see us together and hope that a certain couple is among the ones that do?"

Eirik smirked, though it wasn't a priority in his eyes. "You read my mind."

"Sure. Just give a minute to grab what I need."

Elle disappeared into the house and when she returned, the hat and sunglasses were back on. She brought with her the scent of sunblock.

"Ready."

It didn't take them long to find their way to the large area dedicated to restaurants and little shops.

He let Elle lead the way. Which was how he found himself watching her gaze with longing at clothes and shoes at one of the many stores in the shopping pavilion. The way she looked at the other women who seemed to be laden with so many bags he was amazed they managed to carry it all. It did, however, also create a pang of empathy for Elle in his gut. Judging from her outfit, which consisted of the same shorts from the day before and another crumpled T-shirt, Eirik figured she didn't do much shopping.

He condemned her ex. The cretin made more than enough money to be more than able to splurge on Elle from time to time, at the very least. Instead, this was what he pictured her doing more often than not. Pining for things she'd never own.

Why did he care? Eirik knew he shouldn't, but he did. Enough that he was willing to lay down some major cash right there just to see her smile. Not that he saw her accepting.

But if there was one thing he knew, it was how to manipulate a situation.

"You know, our exes might have an easier time believing that we're together if we actually look the part."

Elle bristled as she scowled at him. "What's that supposed to mean?"

He glanced meaningfully at the displays before returning his gaze to her with a smile. "It means that I'm known to lavish gifts on my lovers."

Her expression only became more mulish. "And Greg knows that I like to pay my own way."

Likes to or has to? Eirik pressed on. "And you said yourself that I'm overbearing and like to get my own way." She turned to glare at him. "Don't you think that if we were a couple I'd at least give you a gift or two?"

"So what are you suggesting?"

"That I buy you a few things." He tilted his head to direct her gaze back to the emerald-green silk dress she'd been staring at for a full five minutes. "Like that."

She balked and shook her head. "I can't. It costs a fortune."

"And mine is at your disposal." He meant it.

Elle gazed up at him, her lips parted in disbelief. "You're not serious."

"Try me." When she challenged him with her eyes, he closed his hands around her shoulders, turned her and pushed her toward the store. "Go and pick out whatever you want and need for the week. The stores here should be able to provide you with whatever you might possibly require. I imagine a few fancy dinners and sunning on the beach or by the pool. Maybe an excursion here or there. Make sure you won't be seen in the same thing twice. I've got something I need to do so I'll meet you back here in a little while."

Elle continued to balk at him so he walked her into the store himself, arm around her shoulder so there was no way she was getting out of it.

He smiled at the nearest shop assistant who blushed as she rushed over.

She gave Elle a cursory glance before letting it settle with a beaming smile on Eirik. "Welcome, how can I help you?"

Eirik smiled. "My girlfriend and I just arrived but our luggage was lost on the way. Can you make sure that my darling, Elle, gets everything she needs for an indulgent week's stay here?"

She pursed her lips at the mention of Elle being his girlfriend, but her expression brightened at the prospect of a big sale. "I'm sure we can accommodate your partner in every way. Is there a budget?"

"None. I want nothing but the best for her." Eirik held up his finger as he strode to the window display and pointed at the dress Elle had been staring at. "But make sure she gets this dress."

The shopkeeper's smile grew as she retrieved the one he'd indicated. "Of course."

Eirik pecked Elle on the top of her head, inhaling her sweet scent. "I'll be back in a little while." He leaned in and kissed her before whispering, "You look like you're going to the gallows. Smile. Have fun."

Still looking a little shell-shocked, Elle nodded. "Thank you."

He winked. "You can thank me later."

A blush rushed into her cheeks before the assistant whisked her away.

That went well. Grinning, Eirik headed to an electronics shop they'd passed earlier.

Elle followed the petite woman through the shop past a variety of displays. More than likely by design. And why wouldn't she? They seemed to cater to a high-end clientele and definitely would have everything she could need. At least apparel wise. If Elle caught a glimpse of something she liked on the way past it would only help speed things up.

"So you'll need everything." The statement was just a reiteration of what Eirik had told the woman, so Elle nodded.

The assistant's gaze traveled over Elle several times before returning to meet hers. "Is there a certain style that you prefer to stick to?"

It was obvious that her current look didn't meet with the woman's approval and Elle fought not to bristle. "Smart-casual should do."

"Very well." She motioned to a seat. "Please relax and let us do the work. Would you like a drink? Sparkling water perhaps? Champagne?"

"Water would be lovely. Thanks."

She received a brisk nod just before she waved over another couple of assistants and had a quick word before they dispersed.

Moments later, Elle sat sipping her water and appraising what seemed like a never-ending parade of clothing.

By the time she'd finished selecting accessories and had stepped into the dressing room to try it all on, Elle had come to the conclusion that she wanted to know more about Eirik. He was as generous with his money as he was with his body. And that intrigued her. She wished that she had her phone so she could at least do a search on him. It was obvious to her that he was a man of means. What he was about to spend on her was no joke and he'd been the one to encourage it. Also, Celina seemed to be a gold digger who would only go for a big target so it made sense that he had money. A lot of it.

It only made her alliance with Greg that much stranger. She had to be with him because of what he may possibly do for her because he certainly didn't have Eirik's cash. Or skills.

What confounded her was for someone who seemed good and kind, Eirik was hell-bent on revenge. There had to be more than his pride at stake. Sure, his ex and Greg had tried to ruin his family. But he could have easily handed the matter over to the police or federal agents or whoever it was you alerted in a situation like this.

Slipping into the gorgeous green silk dress, Elle sighed. How had she managed to find someone so perfect and yet so unattainable? He'd made it clear that they were only together for however long it took for him to get his revenge.

She had to remember that.

In the meantime she should go with it. Maybe even enjoy it. So far this had been the best vacation she'd ever been on.

How sad is that?

Hysterical laughter bubbled up her throat. The best trip she'd ever been on had started with her finding out her fiancé was with another woman. She was now with a man who was pretty much perfect, at least as far as she knew, who was with her out of revenge and wasn't interested in anything more than an island fling.

And she was okay with that. Really. This was the perfect time for her to reprioritize. Reassess. Just start over.

It was obvious the life she had was gone. But why did it have to be a bad thing? She'd put off her own dreams and ambitions for long enough. And for what? Turning this trip into one of self-discovery and fun would be the best thing for her at this point in her life.

What better way to do that than to let loose and enjoy herself with a man like Eirik who seemed to know exactly how to do that?

Knowing that there was an expiry date on their relationship actually made her feel more at ease. There was no time for either of them to lose interest. Not enough time to take each other for granted or fall out of lust.

This is perfect, really.

A perfect relationship.

Yeah, right.

Turning her attention to the present, Elle stared at her reflection in the mirror.

The dress fit like a dream. Elle swished back and forth a little to admire herself in it. It would be perfect for an elegant dinner.

Checking the tag drained the blood from her head and left her a little faint. A quick look at the other tags only made the feeling worse. She couldn't let Eirik spend this kind of cash on her. But there was little to do about it now. She knew enough about Eirik to anticipate that he probably wouldn't let her out of the store without buying something.

With swift, but delicate, care she changed out of the dress and hung it on a separate hook. It took a few agonizing minutes but she weeded out the most expensive of the clothes and added them to the same hook.

What she decided on were a couple of simple dresses, a pair of loose flowing trousers, a blouse to go with it, a plain one-piece bathing suit in sapphire blue and a pair of tan sandals that would go with them all. Satisfied that they would do and that Eirik would be mollified with her choices, she set them aside.

Taking one last look at the dress she'd been mooning over, Elle dropped it onto the massive stack of rejects and opened the door before she changed her mind. "I won't be needing these."

"I think you will." Eirik barged into the already small space and took the clothes from her. Though they were almost forgotten when he saw that she was in nothing but her underwear. "Although, if you wear nothing but what you have on for the rest of our stay, I'd be a very happy man."

It seemed he wasn't satisfied with just looking and, after dropping the clothes on the stool, he brought his hands into play. He rested them on her waist while he caressed all the skin he could just by spreading his fingers.

Eirik's presence sucked up the air and the rest of the space in the little room. Him picking her up as if she weighed no more than a one of the dresses in there made her feel delicate. Though, when he pressed her against the wall, a position that was becoming a fast favorite, everything but burning need was forgotten.

"We're buying everything in here."

The use of 'we' caused her eyes to widen a little. "Are we now?"

Nodding, he smirked. "Do I have to convince you?"

Elle wriggled against him. "Maybe." She'd play his game now, but wasn't going to spend that kind of money on her. Especially when they weren't in a real relationship. Even if they had been, she'd have a problem with him just buying her things.

Elle's resolve faltered somewhat, however, when his lips met the skin between her neck and shoulder.

But who could blame her for losing the ability to think when he was touching her?

His big warm hands turned into the sparking points for heat that bloomed through her, flooding her system in a cascade of heat. But when his mouth met hers hard with need, Elle was lost.

Eirik eased his fingers under her panties, eliciting a tiny squeal of delight from Elle.

"Shhh. You don't want someone coming in and ruining our fun, do you?"

God, no.

Shaking her head, she circled her hips needing the friction again.

Chuckling, Eirik nipped her neck. "Greedy."

And she was.

She would make the most of it while she was able.

Eirik was only too happy to help Elle out. He wasn't sure what he'd been expecting to find when he stepped into the fitting room but finding Elle in her underwear was the best outcome he could imagine. Or damn close to it. But finding her naked in there was just a pipe dream.

Slipping a couple of fingers into her hot, tight body had his already hard cock aching to do the same. He fought back the need to sink into her right then and there since the thought of someone possibly walking by and ruining the moment wasn't something he relished. He knew enough about Elle to know that would ruin the mood for a long while.

Better this way.

She was so petite he was able to hold her against the wall with his hips leaving his hands free to explore.

The vivid blue of something silk caught his eye and he continued to stroke her while he snared it with the fingers of his free hand. She watched with heavy lidded eyes as he bunched it in his hand. Eirik brought it up to caress her cheek. "You're telling me you don't want to feel something so soft and silky against your skin again?"

He slid it down her neck to the sensitive upper curves over her breast. From the way she inhaled and arched into the fabric, he'd have to say that she was sold on that. Just in case she wasn't, Eirik brushed it over one then the other. "What do you think? Wouldn't you miss the sensation of this?"

She nodded.

"Then say you'll buy it."

"All right."

"I was hoping for a little more enthusiasm." Eirik trailed it over her belly so that it whispered over her skin before he kissed her again.

When he pulled back, she was breathless and dazed but nodding. "Yes."

Elle writhed against him. "Please, Eirik. I need you to move...your fingers..."

Eirik brushed his lips against hers. "All in good time. We're still looking at your selection."

She pouted, though it was adorable when she did it. Then a devious glint lit her eyes. What was she up to?

Elle ran her hands down his arms before sliding them up his chest. He could tell from the hesitation and slight tremble in them that she wasn't sure of what she was doing. Her attempting to seduce him was a huge turn-on. That she pushed her boundaries, for him, was more than flattering.

Still, he wouldn't play into her hands right away. In his opinion, the best prizes were hard won.

But when she found her way under his shirt, his best intentions were blasted away with a wave of hunger. The desire for her hadn't been dampened even after the night they'd had. In fact, it might have been stoked more, knowing what she was capable of doing to him.

And, even with them crammed together in a little cubicle while people walked outside not five feet away, the need for her raged.

Elle's hot hands on his chest left blazing trails as she explored. But when she reached the waistband of his trousers, he had to stop her.

"I think we need more time and privacy for that." He chuckled when she scowled at him. "That doesn't mean we can't satisfy you for the moment."

Grinding the palm of his hand against her clit, Eirik smiled. "Think you can keep quiet?"

Elle bit her lip. They both knew that she was quite vocal and she was unsure if she would be able to manage it.

He pressed his lips to hers, whispering, "Let me help," before deepening the kiss. Elle quivered against him as he slid his fingers deeper, crooking them on the pull-out, knowing from the night before that she loved it.

Eirik kept the rhythm steady, the stimulation on her clit light and teasing. He shook from the force it took not to pull out his cock and plunge into her. That it didn't take him long before Elle was crying out into his mouth and clenching on his fingers sent a surge of pride streaking through him. Making sure to draw out her orgasm, Eirik kept it up until she sagged limp and pliant against him.

For a long moment, they stood wrapped around each other. Eirik supported her weight until the strength returned to her knees. The languid afterglow evaporated when there was a light tapping on the door, however.

"Is everything all right in there? Anything I can help with?"

Eyes wide with panic, Elle jammed her foot against the door. "Everything's fine!"

The jovial voice on the other side didn't miss a beat. "Just shout if you need anything."

"I will!" She turned her gaze to him. But when he thought there would a be a decent into panic and despair, Elle started laughing. Giggling uncontrollably, she covered her mouth with her hands to try to muffle the sound.

When it finally died, she still grinned. "I can't believe we just did that!"

"We would have done so much more if it wasn't for all the people milling around," he grumbled.

That only made her giggles start all over again.

Glad that she wasn't castigating herself, Eirik handed her one of the new dresses for her to put on. "I'll take the rest to the till."

When she simply held the dress and stared at him, he knew what was coming. "I don't want any argument. Just think of all this as a thank-you for helping me out."

"It's too much. I've picked out a few things that will do." She motioned at the few items hanging on the peg nearest the door.

Eirik couldn't help but smile. She was totally unlike Celina and some of the other women he'd been associated with. They not only would have taken what was offered but would have gone and tried to buy out the store.

"It's fine. Stop worrying." He grabbed everything, including the clothes she had worn into the store so that she no option but to wear the new dress. "You have five seconds to put that on before I open the door."

"But—"

He put his hand on the door handle. "Four seconds."

"Eirik!" Elle threw the garment over her head and tugged it into place with a second to spare.

He zipped her up before taking a look at her in the mirror. "You look fantastic."

She waved at herself. "It's hard not to in a dress like this."

"Believe me. You only make it look better." He winked. "I'll meet you outside."

By the time he had paid and everything was boxed and bagged, Elle had emerged from the change room appearing put together and calm but a little distracted.

He did notice that she was avoiding everyone's gaze but his. Not wanting her to feel more awkward, Eirik wound an arm around her, bade the women goodbye and led her from the store.

Elle stayed silent for the next few minutes. What could he do to assuage her embarrassment? Asking her if she was okay seemed inadequate. His best bet would be to stay silent until she was ready to talk.

The aimless, quiet walk led them out of the shopping complex out into the sunlight. Aside from narrowing her eyes against the glare of the sun, Elle barely changed her expression. Though he wanted to give her space to have her reaction, Eirik was getting tired of the silent treatment.

By the time they were on the sand and the water lapped within reach of their toes, he'd had enough.

"You don't have anything to say?"

It was at that moment that she seemed to come out of trance. She shook her head hesitantly. "Not really."

Elle didn't look upset, only unfocused.

"What's wrong?"

"Nothing. I was just thinking about music again."

For some reason that eased the tight sensation in his chest. She wasn't upset. She wasn't angry with him. There was no silent treatment. Relief flooded him just while at the same time there was enough confusion to keep him off center. Would she ever cease to amaze him?

He liked that music seemed to be creeping into her thoughts more and more. To him, it signaled that her mind was relaxing. That she was allowing herself to think without restraint. "Speaking of music..." Eirik shuffled the bags until he found the one he was looking for. "I got you this."

Elle took it from him and peered inside. "Eirik, you shouldn't have."

When she didn't take it out, he reached in and retrieved the box holding her new phone and opened it before she tried to protest again. "It's a good phone. I know because it's identical to mine and I made sure that they preloaded it with the best music writing app."

Elle stared up at him for what had to be the umpteenth time since meeting him. How was he forever able to keep her off-kilter? She pushed his hand away. "Thank you, but..." She shook her head.

"Please. I had a hand in destroying your old one."

First the villa, then clothes and now this? Elle wasn't sure what he was trying to do. Was he in all honesty just a giving man or was this just an attempt to buy her loyalties? "If you think you have to give me things so that I'll help you, you really don't need to. I told you I would and I don't go back on my word."

For a moment he looked insulted and Elle was terrified that she'd screwed this up royally.

When she was sure he was going to dump all her things into the ocean and walk away, he shook his head as he gave her a tiny, almost stunned smile. "You're not like other women, are you?"

She glared up at him. "I prefer not to be compared to anyone."

"I meant no offense. Other women I've been acquainted with would be jumping through hoops to have someone buy things for them. You, on the other hand, are the opposite." He grinned. "Unless you're trying a new tactic."

"I think I should punch you for that." But rather than hit him, Elle just laughed. "I guess I'm not the social-climbing, money-grabbing type that you usually associate with."

"I guess not."

"You don't have to sound so upset about it."

"Not at all. I think you're a breath of fresh air."

Yeah, for now. How long before the novelty of strange little me wears off?

Taking a deep breath, she straightened her shoulders. What did it matter? It wasn't like she was looking for another relationship. Didn't she promise herself to just go with it and enjoy herself while it lasted?

Forcing a smile, she took the phone. "Thank you for being so generous and thoughtful."

His smile grew into a grin. "You're welcome."

Elle's heart fluttered when she turned the glossy new phone on and took a look at it. There would be a lot of things she'd have to recover and try to figure out—even with her limited knowledge of technology, she saw it was a fantastic device. And Eirik having one was the best possible endorsement.

"I'm impressed."

He breathed a happy sigh. "I'm glad you like it."

Catching his gaze, she found herself captivated. Why couldn't he be the one for her?

It was a long while before she tore her attention away from him and turned it back to the phone. It was easy to find the app he was talking about. A tap and a microsecond later, she was learning her way around it.

It looked to be the precise thing she needed.

"The app is perfect too. How can I thank you?" The instant the words left her mouth and her eyes met his again, she knew what the answer would be.

At least what she expected to hear from him. Yet again, in true Eirik Mikkelsen style, he turned her world on its ear again with his next words.

"Just write something that will change the world."

Chapter Seven

They walked a meandering path along the waterline. While enjoying the natural beauty of the island, Elle found herself torn between watching the birds dancing on the dazzling azure water and staring at the puzzle of a man next to her. Eirik seemed to sense that she was composing in her head and needed quiet. He contented himself with people watching and checking messages on his phone when he wasn't pointing out interesting scenes. So far he'd only interrupted her thoughts a couple of times. Once for a pod of cavorting dolphins and the other to point out whales breaching. Both times they just watched in silent awe, comfortable and happy with that arrangement.

Elle still couldn't get over just how well they clicked or how contented she was with Eirik. After the turbulent morning, things had settled between them to become as serene as the sea she now stared at in such wonderment.

The man inspired much the same feelings when she looked at him. Some time ago, he'd taken off his shoes and had rolled up the legs of his jeans to facilitate wading in the shallows. Likewise, his sleeves had been rolled up to show off the intriguing shadows on his sculpted forearms. She watched with great interest as he picked up a stone and threw it with explosive force into the ocean. If she hadn't known better, she would have guessed that Eirik had been a part of the island. He looked so at home and natural there.

The breeze toyed with loose tendrils of his hair, begging her to touch them. Elle gave into the temptation and stepped closer to do just that.

Eirik caught her gaze with an easy smile while she tucked the strand behind his ear. "What do you say we get out of this heat and have something to eat? If you're ready, that is."

"Sounds good to me." Elle smirked when he crooked his arm. She looped hers through and smiled up at him. "What did you have in mind?"

"I thought we'd head back to the villa and have something there. Or, if you'd rather, there are restaurants we haven't tried yet…"

Elle shook her head. The prospect of more quiet time was perfect. "Going back to the villa sounds great."

Nodding, he steered them in the right direction. They walked a minute before he asked, "You prefer peace and quiet, don't you?"

"Most of the time, yes." There were times it was unattainable and that didn't bother her too much. But, if given the choice, Elle would almost always choose her own company.

Here and now? She would choose the option that would afford her more time alone with Eirik. To a degree because she was curious and wanted to know more about him. The other part of her knew that even with him around he wasn't going to get in her way or bother her. At least not too much.

And if he did bother her, it was for a very good and often tantalizing reason.

Like helping her reach some pretty spectacular orgasms.

A tremor, almost like an aftershock, rippled through her at just the memory of what he could do to her. What she could do to him. The inferno that burned between them.

It was easy to see how people's minds were clouded by sex. Especially of the caliber they had. Elle found that whenever she wasn't thinking about music she was reliving the blistering memories of them burning up the sheets.

She needed to keep things in perspective. Difficult but necessary.

"Thinking about your music again?"

Elle turned her gaze up to find him watching her. "Something like that." It was a half-truth at best. Being with him inspired the music in her head in addition to a torrent of X-rated thoughts. It wasn't her fault that they often became entangled.

He accepted her reply with a small smile as they walked the rest of the way in companionable silence.

The interior of the villa was a welcome respite from the sultry heat of the day. Taking off her sunglasses and hat, Elle sighed with relief using the latter to fan the cool air into her face. She'd completely lost track of how long they'd been out there.

Eirik put the bags down by the door and headed to the kitchen to retrieve bottles of water. He sauntered over to offer her one, which she took with a grateful smile. "Anything in particular you want for lunch?"

His phone pinged while she shook her head. "Something light."

Nodding, he pulled out his phone. "I'll get on that in a sec."

Elle bit back the urge to ask what was so interesting on his screen. What right did she have to ask? He fired off a quick text before calling one of the restaurants and ordering their food.

Once that was done, he winked at her. "Lunch is on its way."

He looked quite pleased with himself. So much so Elle had to wonder what else was going on.

Dropping back onto the couch, Eirik dragged her with him. "I've found out where our exes are going to be dining tonight."

So, it's the possibility of seeing his ex that has him so smug.

Not sure of what to think of that, Elle nodded as she stared out at the cloudless sky. "So you're formulating a plan of some sort, I take it."

"I'd say it's a variation on your plan, actually." He ran his finger along the column of her throat.

His touch caused electricity to race up her nerves to fizzle and pop in her brain. She had a plan?

When she said nothing, Eirik kept going. "You know, the one where you show up looking fabulous and crush your ex under your stiletto heel?"

Elle vaguely remembered saying something along those lines. "I don't think I said anything about crushing him with my heel, though."

"I thought that was implied," he chuckled, tracing lazy circles on her skin.

She followed the impulse to stretch out and let him use her body as an instrument for his wandering fingers.

Eirik traced the line of her neck downward, following the trail with his lips. His tongue.

"You smell fantastic," he whispered against her skin. "And taste even better."

He did too. She tugged him up enabling her to capture his mouth with hers.

Elle wasn't just going to let him have his way this time, however. He had had all the fun in the change room. Now it was her turn to play.

She twisted around to push against his chest. Eirik dropped easily onto his back, an intrigued look in his eyes. Elle didn't hold it for too long. She didn't want to lose her nerve. And having him bore into her mind with those eyes of his might do just that.

Slowly, she unbuttoned his shirt, taking a moment to appreciate every bit of skin that was revealed with each button until she was able to push the fabric apart and his chest was bare to her gaze. His body was one she would never get bored of looking at. Or feeling. But since she would never get the chance to find out, she would make the most of it now.

Elle dragged her hands over his muscled stomach, to graze his hard pecs. Everything about the man was solid.

Meanwhile, Eirik lay under her, letting her do as she pleased. He watched her interested in what she would do next. Without judgment. From the ridge that was forming under her ass, she knew he enjoyed what she was doing.

She wriggled against his erection, earning a groan. He attempted to rock her on his lap to get more stimulation, but she resisted.

Laughing, she leaned forward to graze his lips with hers again. "If you keep that up, I'm going to stop."

Eirik smirked, putting up his hands in a gesture that said she was in control. The mischievous glint in his eyes did have her wondering just how much he would take before his control snapped.

Shimmying down his body, she flicked a tongue over one nipple, enjoying watching it harden before she did the same to the other. She glided her tongue down his chest and stomach until she reached the waistband of his jeans.

The bulge of his straining hard-on through the fabric had her mouth watering. It took a moment of her running the tips of her fingers along the edge to work up the nerve to slide her fingers under the fabric and flick the button loose.

Unzipping the jeans, she didn't realize she was holding her breath until the tab could go no further. The clearly defined ridge of him hidden by the thin fabric of his underwear jerked under her gaze.

Elle nipped her bottom lip between her teeth while she eased his clothes over his hips. Until he was exposed to her hungry gaze.

Oh, god.

He was huge. Not a new revelation, but being face to face with him sent a tendril of awe sweeping through her. He was long and thick and absolutely beautiful. Wanting to feel him, Elle closed her hand around him. Or at least tried to.

"Elle," he moaned.

She smiled when he pushed into her hand, no long able to keep still. The fact that she had a man as big and in control as Eirik gasping and trembling was a rush. She loved that he was helpless when she did nothing more than touch him.

Or when she used her mouth.

Elle flicked her tongue over the broad head of his cock, licking up the bead of pre-cum that had formed. At his groan, she pumped her hand up and down his length, taking the head into her mouth. She swirled her tongue around him, thrilled at how tense he'd become under her. After their little interlude in the change room, Elle knew he would be wound up.

How long would it take her to get him to come?

Tilting her head so she could hold his gaze, Elle bobbed. Her movement was slow and experimental at first then settled into a rhythm that Eirik, very vocally, approved of.

Her hint that he was getting close was he slid his big hands into her hair, holding her still against the shallow thrusts he made into her mouth. Elle knew that he was trying to be gentle, but with each plunge into her mouth he got a little deeper and the trembling grew.

Using both hands on his shaft, Elle concentrated her efforts on the head, sucking and flicking her tongue against the sensitive spot just underneath.

He tightened his grip on her hair as he shoved himself past her lips. For a tense second there was stillness. The battle he waged with his body was lost, however, when he came with a shout.

She licked, sucked and swallowed taking everything he gave her. It wasn't until his entire body seemed to lose all its energy and he dropped his hands from her hair that she eased up.

Elle gave him a final lick, causing Eirik to jerk in reaction.

Grabbing her hand with a laugh, he tugged her over him so that he could hold her.

Lying sprawled over him with her head on his chest, Elle smiled. Satisfaction thrummed through her at being able bring him the same pleasure he gave her.

For a long while there was no other sound but the thundering of his heart and his heavy breath as he recovered.

Before his heart slowed back into its steady pace, he let hands wander. Over her back. Her ass. Slowly. Purposefully. It didn't take him long to drag the dress up and out of the way of his seeking hands. Under her, his cock showed signs of renewing interest.

Elle smirked against his chest. Their hunger for each other seemed insatiable. As if his touch wasn't enough, knowing that he wanted her again sent throbbing heat coursing through her to pool between her thighs.

Eirik closed his hands around her waist and lifted her easily.

Swiping aside the barrier of her clothing, Elle sighed with delight as he lowered her onto his erection. He made sure her progress was slow, almost agonizing, until she was seated on him fully.

"So deep," she whispered.

Holding her in place, Eirik sat up to meet her lips with his. He turned so that his feet were planted on the floor, and surged upward.

Gasping into his mouth, Elle hung on while he set a deep and grinding rhythm. Eirik's grip on her hips tightened as she rocked and bounced against him. On him.

Still, wanting it to last forever, she fought against the rising tide of sensation.

It only prompted him to push himself deeper into her. Harder. Eirik kissed her again, brushing his tongue against hers.

Tingling in her toes forced her to curl them while she tried to hang on.

"Come on, Elle," he whispered. "I can feel it starting to take over. Don't you want to come for me?" He pumped into her. "I want to feel your hot little body squeeze me tight."

That was it.

Wailing, Elle came in a flare of pleasure. Bright white sparks blinded her as she rode out her orgasm.

As the world refocused, she was only vaguely aware of the look of triumph that crossed his face just before he exploded.

Elle stared down at him while he slowly smiled at her. As always, sex with Eirik was astounding. She wanted to believe that this was more than just great chemistry. In her bones, she felt this was different than anything she had experienced with anyone else. How could you mesh with someone this well and not have it mean something more?

She melted into him after they fell back onto the couch to catch their breaths. Laying there tangled together felt so right.

Wouldn't it be perfect just to fall asleep right there?

To her dismay, there was a knock at the door that kept the urge from becoming a reality.

Eirik gave her a wolfish grin before he helped her off him and lurched to his feet. He righted his clothes with a few deft movements and waited until he got the nod from her before he headed to the door.

Giggling, Elle made a quick dash to the bathroom to collect herself and tidy up.

By the time she returned Eirik stood waiting with a dome-covered tray in one hand and his other arm curled around a sweating ice bucket. "Where would you like to eat?"

Not really wanting to be out in the heat again, Elle let her gaze wander around the room for a suitable spot but found none that didn't require too much effort to get to. She waved at the coffee table. "Why not right here?"

"Why not, indeed." He put his burden down with a smile. "I'll get some glasses."

Elle slipped between the couch and the table to sit crossed-legged on the floor while Eirik busied himself finding plates, glasses and cutlery.

She waited for him to come back to reveal what he had ordered, watching him all the while.

He noticed her studying him when he returned. "What?"

"Nothing."

Eirik took his place across from her. "No, really."

"I was just thinking that you seem so at home here." In addition to wishing this was her reality.

"I'll admit I like it here. Who wouldn't? This place has it all." He let his gaze flick to her before lifting the dome. "Or is it the company that makes everything about this place that much better?"

Heat flooded her cheeks. Still, she couldn't stop looking at him. There was so much about him she didn't know and yet she would probably be able to etch his body from memory at this point.

"You're still staring." She hadn't even noticed him flit a glance her way as he filled their plates with salad and fish then deftly poured the wine. Sitting down, he twined a wayward lock of hair behind his ear. From the way he locked his gaze with hers, Elle knew he was waiting for her to comment.

Picking up her glass, she took a sip. "I'm trying to figure you out, I guess."

"What about me has you so puzzled?"

Elle lifted a shoulder. "I don't know…"

Eirik settled back and took a sip, watching her all the while.

While she couldn't fathom him, Eirik seemed able to delve straight into her mind through her eyes. It was though he saw everything about her. Her thoughts, her feelings. Yet doing the same to him didn't work for her at all.

Frustrated, she sighed. "Why the beard and the hair?"

He didn't see that coming from the way he frowned. "What's wrong with it?"

"Nothing." Absolutely nothing. "I'm just intrigued."

He put his wine down. "I suppose I just like to be different. Why should I be like everyone else?"

"I never said you should be." Elle poked at the delicious-looking food with her fork, her appetite waning more with every word. "Forget I said anything."

He glowered at the food. Had his hunger disappeared as well? "Would you rather I look like every other man out there? Or like your ex?"

She put her fork down. "When did I say that? All I asked was about your choice."

"And you don't like what I've chosen." His tone told her he'd made up his mind.

"What I don't like is that a smart and beautiful man like you has chosen to hide — to mask — himself from the world even when he's telling everyone he doesn't care. And is willing to push everyone away to prove it." She shoved her plate back but picked up her glass when she stood. "I've got to get ready for dinner. I've got people to try and impress. That takes time."

Elle got up, seeking the solace of her room.

Eirik spent the rest of the afternoon brooding along the waterline until the heat drove him back indoors. The plan to have a delicious lunch accompanied by delightful conversation and some light plotting had gone to hell when Elle had asked about his appearance. He knew he was the one who was out of line. He'd jumped down her throat when she had said nothing wrong.

He was well aware that he was touchy when it came to discussing himself. Elle had been nothing but amazing this whole time and she didn't deserve being talked to like he had.

Guilt gnawed at his gut. He had to make it up to her. What amazed him was that after only knowing her for such a short amount of time, Elle had become a shining point in his life. A tantalizing breath of fresh air.

Eirik was annoyed to realize that everything he came up with paled in comparison to what he felt he owed her. He knew if he bought her anything, it would be seen to be a bribe. Anything involving throwing his cash around would be a crass and empty gesture, anyway. He had to show her his remorse in a way she would appreciate and know was true.

Which led them him to where he was now.

He'd gone and bought a new suit, had spent longer than usual prepping only to find himself standing outside her bedroom door staring at the wood while he tried to formulate an apology. Not to mention muster the courage to knock.

Getting Elle out and having a good time was the main goal of the night. That he would be killing two birds with one stone was just icing on the cake. From their conversations he got the impression that she didn't get out much. Or when Henning had deigned to take her out it was for boring business functions. Most of her time seemed to have been spent waiting around for her ex. As far as Eirik was concerned, she had wasted too much of her life on that loser.

The little digging he'd done earlier told him that their exes would be dining at the best restaurant in the resort, which came into perfect alignment with his plans.

He would help her loosen up and get back at Henning at the same time. It was a win-win situation in his eyes.

Eirik looked forward to spending time with Elle. The more he got to know her, the more intrigued he became. Sweet and sultry, funny and charming, intelligent and witty — Elle was a great woman to be on vacation with.

The strange thing was, he was beginning to imagine her in other situations. Waking up next to her back at his flat in Oslo. Watching movies entwined on the couch after a long day. Cooking dinner together. Long candlelit baths. Lying in bed limbs entangled talking about everything and anything. Meeting her at the airport after some time apart and the inevitable incendiary reunion...

Only Elle was on the rebound and a relationship between them after a breakup so traumatic probably wasn't on the cards.

In the meantime, he'd be the guy to help her get over Henning. And all the perks that came with that were hard to complain about.

What he found odd was that in spite of all the time they'd spent naked together, he couldn't bring himself to just waltz into her room uninvited. Especially not after what had happened at lunch.

He knocked and waited, his heart in his throat, for her to acknowledge it.

But she didn't.

"Elle?" Eirik knocked again but when Elle didn't respond, his heart started jackhammering. Was something wrong?

Pushing the door open, he heard nothing. Not the shower, not movement. "Elle?"

For too many heartbeats, he thought she had taken off. It made no sense. Why would she after they'd had such a good time together? Unless she had gone back to Henning because of what had happened at lunch...

Illogical all-consuming rage surged through him. Even more cause to destroy the runt. And he would. Tear him apart. Atom from atom.

Movement from outside the French doors caught his eye. Deep-red fabric caught on the sea breeze danced on the other side of the glass.

She hadn't left.

Relief quickened Eirik's long steps across the room and propelled him through the opened doors to find Elle, at the railing, staring out at the water.

Only when he approached her side did he realize that she was on her phone, writing music on the app, oblivious to everything else.

Finding her so focused made him almost regret having to drag her away.

Not wanting to startle her, he stepped to the railing next to her. "Elle?"

"Huh?" She blinked as if seeing him for the first time. Then she lowered her eyebrows, clearly fixing her thoughts on him. "Sorry. I lost track of time."

"I see that." Eirik brushed a loose wisp of hair out of her eyes. "Are you busy? Would you rather skip dinner? It would be easy to order something in."

Her eyes softened, but she shook her head. "You went to all the trouble of tracking where they would be." Elle gazed down at herself. "And buying me this dress."

"I'll buy you another." He was more than ready to kick off his shoes and drag her over to a sun lounger to settle in to let her write to her heart's content, but Elle was already putting the phone into her purse and fussing with her dress.

With a flick of her hair over her shoulder, she smiled at him. "How do I look?"

"Every man will be jealous of me tonight."

Eirik was charmed by the way she flushed red from the curves of her breasts to the roots of her hair.

"Stop it."

"It's the truth." He took her hand and tugged her close. "You are the most beautiful woman in every room, dressed up or not."

When she tried to argue, Eirik lowered his head to capture her lips with his, silencing her to great effect.

It was the truth. Her warmth and kindness only added to her beauty in his eyes. All her qualities came together in a very alluring package that he was finding very hard not to covet for his own.

At least in the meantime he'd pretend she was his.

Licking her taste from his lips, Eirik wound an arm around her waist. "Shall we?"

Knees wobbling more than a little, Elle was glad of Eirik's strong arm steadying her on the path as they walked.

She knew he was only trying to build up her confidence when he told her things like she was the most beautiful woman in the room. He needed her to appear happy and comfortable with him. Which, unaccountably, she was. It usually took her quite a while to open up to someone.

With Eirik, it just seemed to easy. They complemented one another well. And not only in bed. Just the thought of how well they meshed there heated her body. The longing to get him naked again almost took her breath away.

She shook it off. Since when had she let lust rule over her?

Since when had sex been good enough to take over her thoughts?

Since Eirik.

His rich voice drew her out of her reverie. "You seem deep in thought. Thinking about your music again?"

"Something like that." Was it merely a coincidence that the melodies had returned full force since meeting him? It was worth a ponder. But right now she had to get her head out of the clouds and into the game. "So what's the plan for tonight?"

"We go to dinner and have a good time."

Seemed simple enough. "That's it?"

His chuckle rumbled through him. "If you want to complicate it, I'd love to hear your plan."

Elle gazed up at him. "We'll play it by ear, I guess."

He replied with a smile. It seemed that the idea was acceptable to him as well.

"I'm sorry about lunch. I didn't mean to be an ass."

Patting his arm, she shrugged. "It's okay, really. I shouldn't have said anything."

"You can say whatever you want. It's my fault for..." He sighed. "It's my fault."

It dawned on her. Eirik took too much to heart. Everything became his doing. But why? Elle wanted to know everything about this enigmatic man. Especially what made him tick.

She stepped in front of him, halting his steps. "Before we forget it happened, I just want you to know that there isn't a thing about you that I dislike or would change. So let it drop, okay?"

He nodded, though from the glint in eye he wasn't about to any time soon. Eirik pressed a gentle kiss to her lips.

Saying nothing more, they started walking again.

Eirik relaxed little by bit little during their stroll along the winding paths.

Whoever designed the resort had a wonderful eye and a romantic heart. The fixtures that lit the winding path flickered from within with faux candlelight and provided little pools of warm light. Just enough to see while keeping the atmosphere dreamy.

That's what all this felt like. A dream. One that she would wake from any moment now. Which only intensified the need in her to make every moment count.

By the time they arrived at the restaurant, Elle wished they would keep walking until they circled back to the villa where he would strip her bare and take her back to bed. There, she'd happily stay until they had to burst this little bubble.

A day she was already coming to rue.

The hostess at the restaurant either already knew who Eirik was or was simply reacting to his presence, because the moment they strolled in, she snapped into action. With a wide smile and fawning eyes, she led the way to their secluded table in an area on the balcony with what appeared to be the best view in the restaurant. They would be alone but everyone in the restaurant, and on the beach, would be able to see them.

Eirik had put a lot of thought into everything. Including the fact that they would be arriving just at the same moment Greg and Eirik's ex would receive their meals and see them walk in.

Elle put on a serene smile as she let Eirik steer her through the maze of tables. Not once did his gaze stray from her, navigating the dining room on what appeared to be pure instinct. The daggers that were their exes' gazes bore into her back while she took her seat. Grateful that Eirik positioned her so that her view was of the ocean, she ignored the prickling feeling at the back of her neck and watched the sparkle of the water. She got the feeling that she would be looking at it all that much with Eirik sitting in front of her.

He settled into his chair with a smile. The hostess rattled off her speech about how happy she was they were there and listed the specials, but Eirik paid her little mind. All his focus stayed on Elle.

Once the woman realized that Eirik wasn't about to spare her a glance, she left them to make their selections. He took one of Elle's hands in his making it easy to believe he couldn't bear not being skin to skin any longer.

It was just for show. She chanted in her mind several times just to make sure it stuck. He was a phenomenal actor. *Remember, it's all an act.*

She had to make sure she kept up. Linking her fingers with his, she picked up the menu with her free hand and began to peruse.

"What are you thinking of having?" he asked.

A big drink would ease my parched throat and calm the churning nausea because I can feel our exes are watching us? "I don't know. Maybe a salad?"

He chuckled. "You don't come all this way for a salad." Eirik scooted his seat over so that they were side-by-side then used her shoulder as a chin rest while he looked at her menu.

Amused, Elle laughed. "You do have one of your own, you know."

"Yes, I do. But I'd rather look at yours." He released their linked fingers to graze them up her arm and under her hair to caress the nape of her neck. "It's much more interesting than mine."

She giggled even though goosebumps prickled her skin at his touch. Unable to help herself, Elle leaned into his hand. "Why don't you choose?"

"What about I get a little of everything and see what we like?"

"Sounds good to me." Everything he said sounded good to her. "But I get to pick the wine."

Laughing, Eirik nodded and waved over a waiter. "Whatever you like."

With the order made, there was nothing left to do but wait. Eirik drew tingling patterns on her nape, soothing her and teasing her senses all at the same time.

It occurred to her that she knew next to nothing about him while feeling like she'd known him for years at the same time. Elle had meant to google him but had been too preoccupied with her music. She would do so when she next got the chance. For now, it wouldn't hurt to ask him a little about himself. He'd been open enough so far...

"So where do you call home, Eirik?"

He raised his eyebrows a fraction in surprise and froze his fingers against her skin. She supposed it was because this was the most personal thing she'd asked him thus far.

The slow circles at the base of her neck resumed. "Oslo, mostly. Though I travel frequently for work."

"Oslo, nice! And what do you do?"

"A little of this and that." He gave her an arched look. "What's with all the questions?"

What *was* with all the questions? "It would be good to know a little bit about each other don't you think? In case we get caught apart and people ask questions." The excuse sounded lame to her own ears.

He leveled his gaze at her. "I suppose. Though I don't foresee us getting separated. Unless you want some time to yourself."

She fought to keep her voice even. "That's not what I'm saying. I just thought we should keep all our bases covered."

Why was she so nervous? It was just a little chitchat. She'd asked more of people she'd known for only minutes during one of Greg's boring business dinners. What made it so hard to talk to Eirik?

Because she didn't want anything to get weird. To change.

What they had was good though not for the long run. What did it matter if she knew anything about him? Other than the fact that he wasn't a homicidal maniac and was incredible in bed, she didn't need to know anything else because it wasn't going to go anywhere.

"You know what? Forget I asked anything." It was like divine intervention when the waiter returned with their wine at that moment and gave her a moment's reprieve.

She took a long sip.

"No, don't do that." Eirik tipped her chin to look at him. "Ask me anything."

"I don't know what to ask now."

He smiled with encouragement. "Well I told you where I live, so it's only fair you tell me where you call home.

"Vancouver. At least for the past few years."

"Before that?"

"London."

His smile grew. "I thought I caught a hint of an English accent."

"It sticks with you, I guess." She laughed. "Have you ever made your way to either city?"

"Quite a few times, in fact. Perhaps you could show me around if I ever find myself there again?"

As if she would say no to that. "Just give me a call."

His smile broadened more. "I'll make sure to do that."

"So what do you do? Besides being a handsome, avenging heartbreaker?"

Leaning back, he regarded her evenly. "According to who?"

Elle wasn't sure of her footing on the topic. The guarded gleam in his eyes put her a little on edge.

"According to you." Because wasn't that what mattered?

"I'm actually surprised that you haven't searched me on the internet."

"And if I had? What would I have found?"

In what looked to her to be a stalling tactic, he took a sip of his wine before answering. "Rumors. Conjecture. A lot of rubbish, really."

She didn't care what the internet or what anyone else said about him. Elle knew her opinion. She wanted to know what he thought about himself. What he was willing to tell her.

"So back to my original question. Who is Eirik, according to you?"

"Does it matter what I think?" He drew his fingers down, eliciting tingles along her spine. "Do you think I'm a good man?"

Did she? She was here with him aiding in his quest to get revenge on a scheming ex. Considering what he said she had done, and Elle believed him on that, she couldn't blame him. And he was helping her get back at Greg too. While in the meantime, making this trip one to remember for the rest of her life. He'd been kind and generous, fun and sexy.

So was he a good man? In her opinion? Yes.

"I believe so."

Her answer seemed to lift a weight off his shoulders. What she thought mattered so much to him?

"Thank you."

Were there so many that felt he wasn't? Elle wanted to ask but refrained. Maybe if they got to know each other better she would hazard that one.

"I know you have more questions." Eirik leveled his gaze at her, his earlier turmoil nowhere to be seen. "Depending on who you talk to, you'd get a different opinion. Obviously. I'm not friends with everyone in the world."

"No one is."

"Exactly."

Still, she got the feeling that the views of some weighed more than others. And the ones that mattered didn't see him through rose-colored lenses. It seemed an internet search later that night was at the top of the list of things to do if she was going to learn anything about him.

She forced a sunny smile when she saw the waiter returning with a brimming tray.

Once it was all placed on the table, it was clear that, though the portions were small, there was just such a huge variety they were never going to make it through everything.

"Think you'll be able to sample a bit of everything?" Eirik winked at her.

"I'll certainly try." Not that she knew where to start.

"Taste this." Eirik took it upon himself to spear a plump shrimp on his fork and present it to her. "It's a personal favorite."

From the look and the delicious scent wafting up from it, Elle wagered it would become something she loved, too. When he refused to give her the fork, Elle was forced to take a bite as he held it. She was hooked from the first taste.

"Told you it was good."

"Good? It's incredible." She took up her own fork and went for another. "I take it you come here often."

He lifted his shoulder a bit and dropped it. "My first trip, actually. I had that yesterday."

Laughing, she chewed. "And just like that it became a favorite?"

Eirik held her gaze. "I'm a man who knows what he likes."

Heat rushed through Elle at the combination of his words and the soul-deep look he gave her. Licking her lips, Elle took a slow breath and then a bite. Chewing with slow and methodical bites, she forced herself to remember how to swallow without choking.

Chew, swallow, sip wine. Smile. Over and over again. Even then she barely got her parched throat and mouth to form words properly.

Elle cleared her throat. "So what's the plan after we're done here?"

"We're going back to the villa where I can peel that dress off you and I'm going to find every spot on your body that makes you squeal with pleasure."

So much for eating. Elle scarcely remembered how to breathe.

Eirik enjoyed the way her cheeks flushed and her eyes dilated at his suggestion. He would make sure that night would be one to remember. Not that every moment with Elle hadn't been amazing so far.

He hadn't meant to say it out loud. But once he had, Eirik knew it was going to be something he would relish making come true.

The questions she asked had thrown him a bit. Was she trying to get to know him better? Was it true interest? What would she think if she knew the truth? He was the family embarrassment. The one who was invited to functions where all the Mikkelsens were needed because they had no other choice.

Would she think less of him?

Did it matter?

For some reason, the answer to that was a resounding 'yes'. For someone he'd only known a short time, Elle's opinion of him mattered. And he wanted to keep it a positive one. The fact that she hadn't searched for him online yet was interesting. Maybe she hadn't needed to know more about him and was just asking out of need for conversation. Whatever her reasoning, she would more than likely check him out now.

The truth should come from him and not the piles of shit on gossip sites.

Later.

Watching Elle now, he noted her nervousness. He couldn't let her give up on the meal. Not with the very busy night he imagined.

Reaching for his fork, he scooped up whatever was in reach and positioned it at her mouth. "Eat."

Her indignation and perhaps a little fluster rose at the command. The heat that flowed between them was palpable and when he'd made the comment about the coming evening, Eirik knew that it had blasted away thoughts of all else. It was hard for him to focus and he imagined it was the same for her.

But the evening was young and they needed to build up their strength for what was sure to be another acrobatic night.

So he focused on feeding her for the most part, himself now and then, and stifling the insistent and growing need to drag her back to the villa and the rest of the world be damned.

As he fed Elle a decadent, creamy spoonful of key lime pie, he got a bit of cream on her lip. Unable to stop himself, Eirik leaned in to lick if off, kissing Elle in the process. The mingled taste of her and the dessert had to be one of the most sinful things he'd ever experienced. He would have gone back for more but there was a clatter across the room that drew their attention out of their little bubble.

They turned in unison to see was a flash of familiar blonde hair and a stomping of stilettos before an apologetic and embarrassed-looking Henning abruptly got up to follow. Not before giving them a long speculative, if accusing, glare.

Eirik had forgotten the other objective of the night had been to provoke their exes. From the look of surprised amusement on Elle's face, she had completely lost sight of the plan as well. Adding to that, seeing Celina incensed and unafraid to show it while the sad little man trailed her out of the restaurant had both tickled her.

"I guess we annoyed them." Elle flipped her hair over her shoulder and turned her focus back to the food. "Goal accomplished."

So then why had her expression slowly morphed into dejection? Had she seen the way her ex had fallen over himself to appease Celina? Knowing what he did about Elle's past relationship, Eirik doubted Elle would have received the same treatment.

Did that bother her?

The ass wasn't worth thinking about.

Eirik waved over the waiter. "We're ready for coffee."

Elle gave him a watery glance but said nothing.

And it pissed him off. After what that louse had done to her, she got upset over seeing him fawning over another woman? Eirik knew that wasn't the only thing bothering him about the whole situation. His pride was dented over the fact that she was still mooning over her ex after having been with him. After what he had considered to be a good time. No, a superb time. They'd clicked on just about every level and yet seeing her ex had soured her mood enough to affect his.

He called back the waiter and growled, "Make that the check."

Elle's speculative gaze met his. Was that surprise? Disappointment? A mix of those and a little of something else? He wasn't sure what he was seeing and he didn't get the chance to analyze before she dropped her gaze to her wine glass.

Then downed the remainder in one gulp.

What was going on in her head?

What the hell was going on in his? Never had he let anyone get under his skin the way Elle had. What was so insane about it was that she mattered. Her opinions, her well-being, her thoughts, it all affected him.

Elle mattered.

The realization was unsettling to say the least. It was the sex. The mind-blowing, jaw-dropping, very addictive sex. With Elle it was sublime but would lose its luster like everything else at the end of the day.

In the meantime, he wouldn't let it addle his mind. Derail him.

He'd been losing focus because of her already. He was here for revenge, not a holiday. The fact that Celina had left the restaurant angry was a coincidence. He had nothing to do with it directly when he should have been puppeteering the whole thing, ensuring a satisfying outcome.

Instead, he'd been flirting and imagining getting Elle into bed again.

As he'd been doing far too often the past few days.

And now he was doing that again even though she was clearly mooning over her ex.

What a sap he was.

Needing to put some space between them, Eirik stood the instant the check hit the table. Throwing down a stack of bills, he glared at Elle.

He didn't miss the tremble in her fingers when she put her glass down, got to her feet and gathered her things.

Without waiting for him, however, she turned toward the stairs on the side of the balcony to descend onto the sand.

Torn between leaving her to the night or following her like a puppy, Eirik found himself trailing behind her into the semi-darkness. Though he was irritated with her, there was no way he'd allow her to wander around in the dark alone.

Elle hadn't seemed to notice him when he caught up with her. She strolled without purpose through the sand, her mind obviously elsewhere. The most probable subject being her loser ex.

It infuriated him that she would waste any time thinking about Henning. That she squandered the last few years with him. And that she still concerned herself over his affairs now.

Did she have so little pride?

Wanting to shake some sense into her, Eirik shoved his hands into his pockets and growled, "Does it bother you so much?"

She jumped a little, gave him a startled glance before nodding. "Yes."

"Why?" He didn't try to hide the angry edge to his voice. Why would she care so much about her ex?

He voice was soft, almost lost in the darkness. "Because I want to know everything about you and it scares me."

Eirik stopped dead in his tracks. *What?* "I'm not sure I heard you right."

"You really want me to say it again?" She scowled and turned to look back at the water. "It weirds me out that I want to know more about you even though I just came out of a relationship and I know for a fact this isn't going to last. That I think about you constantly and, while my imagination keeps heading back to bed, I want to do more than just that with you. On top of it all, I can't even focus on a simple plan to annoy Greg and your ex because I'm so preoccupied with you."

Unable to stop himself, Eirik circled around her, uncaring that in doing so, he strode into the water. He stared at her a scant moment before he leaned in, cupped her cheeks and kissed her.

It was hard and biting and leeched strength from their bodies and the air from their lungs.

When he finally needed to breathe, he drew back to see her staring up at him sleepy-eyed and gasping for breath. He took her hand and tugged her so she walked side-by-side with him. "Come."

Eirik fought to keep his pace slow. He too needed to get some things off his chest before they got back to the villa and all thoughts were burned away.

"I'm sorry I asked so many questions. I didn't mean to annoy you."

That's what she thought? Feeling like an ass, he shook his head. "I think we got our wires crossed. I was irritated because I believed you were moping over your ex."

That caused a titter of laughter to come bubbling from her.

He bristled. "What?"

"That's absurd. You really think I'd care what he does after what he's done to me?"

If she didn't think him a fool for worrying about her, Eirik didn't care. "I don't want you to get upset by him." Or anything else.

"You don't have to worry about that." She fell silent for a few steps. "So what's so horrible about you that you don't want to tell me?"

"It's not horrible, per se. More vexing." He sighed and looked at her. "Would it salve your pride to know that I want you to think well of me?"

He caught the flash of her smile.

"It would. But from what I know about you it can't be that bad."

Couldn't it? "I suppose it depends on your point of view."

"So are you going to tell me or should I start guessing? Just to warn you, I have a vivid imagination."

Eirik didn't doubt it. "Let's just say I have a contentious relationship with my family."

She nodded understandingly. "Lots of people do. That's nothing to be ashamed of."

"It's the other way around. I'm the one they're embarrassed of."

Elle turned to him, dragging him to a stop. "Whatever for?"

"Name it. How I live my life, who I associate with, my business sense…" He shrugged. "My family built our name, our wealth, on construction. New buildings, soaring architecture. That sort of thing."

"So what does that have to do with you?"

"My brothers and I are expected to uphold the family tradition. Nils and Finn have never deviated from the path set out by our father. I, on the other hand, can't seem to do anything right."

Contrary to what he feared, showing her his vulnerable side only strengthened her attraction to Eirik. Now that he was opening up, Elle knew that it would change things. She hoped that it was for the better.

Elle gave him what she hoped he'd interpret to be an encouraging smile. "I think you should do what's right for you. If that doesn't please some people, then maybe they shouldn't be a part of your life."

Smiling he tugged her into walking again. "Spoken like someone who's seen the light."

Elle nodded. If he was able to speak about the hard things then so could she. "Until recently, I hadn't realized just how much I'd closed myself from the world and all because it was what Greg wanted. It was always about what Greg wanted. I didn't even notice that I'd given up making decisions for myself…for anything. Everything. Before him, it was my parents and having to live up to their lofty expectations. By their rules. My entire life has been dictated by what other people wanted or expected of me."

Eirik's hand tightened on hers in a comforting squeeze.

It felt so good to talk it out, especially with someone who obviously understood and didn't judge.

"In a way, it's a good thing that he did what he did. I'm free for the first time. I can do whatever I want whenever I want." She stared up at him. "To hell with everyone else."

She was the one to drag him down this time. She chose to be with him. Chose to do this here and now.

Elle pressed her mouth to his, parted his lips and dipped her tongue inside.

Eirik lifted her, hiked her skirt up enough to free her legs and to wind them around him while giving his hands access to her thighs and butt. The feel of him so big and strong against her was so life affirming. So thrilling.

She broke the kiss. "Let's go back to the villa."

"You read my mind." Eirik started walking, carrying her as if it was something everyone did.

Laughing, she gave him a light shove at his hard shoulders. "Put me down." Not that she wanted him to heed her command.

"Why?" He only held onto her with a more secure grip and bullheadedly kept going.

Still grinning she cocked her head to look at him. "I don't know. Maybe for the sake of propriety?"

"There's hardly anyone around. And those who are don't matter."

The subtext being that they were the only ones that mattered to him.

He was right. Who cared about anyone else?

It was agonizing how slow the progress they made toward the villa was because of the frequent pauses they made when neither was able to wait for another kiss. Another caress. He glided his hands under her clothes while he walked, igniting her skin just at the same time as her desire.

By the time they arrived at the villa, Elle trembled from head to toe, glad that Eirik had kept hold of her, because there was no way she would have made it back without an embarrassing tumble or two into the sand.

The only reason she even realized they had reached the villa was because Eirik pressed her against the door while he kissed her and searched his pocket for the keycard. His fumble with the door and how he managed to unlock it and push it open without letting her go, amazed her.

Back in their little haven again, Elle relinquished control over her need to be skin to skin with him. Grabbing the edges of his shirt, she tore them apart to get her hands underneath. It wasn't enough. Needing to feel him against her, Elle broke the kiss so she could pull her dress off.

Anticipating her move, Eirik already had her unzipped and rucked the skirt up around her waist. In a flash, it was off and tossed aside. Being left in only the tiniest silk bra and panties would do for the moment.

As long as she felt his skin on hers, nothing else mattered.

Kissing her again with a ferocity that caused the ache deep inside to intensify, Eirik strode to the nearest bedroom — his — and laid her on the wide bed.

He watched her with those piercing eyes as if daring her to move. Not that she was able. Elle only seemed able to stare at him and gaze covetously at every inch of skin that came into view when he tore his clothing off in rough, rending jerks.

Moonlight slashed over him, giving her glimpses when she would rather have seen it all. But it was the expression on his face that held her rapt. The intense need was clear. Lust knocked the breath from her lungs and kicked up the beat of her heart.

Eirik tugged her panties down her legs then tossed them over his shoulder before gliding his hands up her body to remove the bra too. When she was finally bare, Eirik wasted no time in tugging her to him, lifting her hips and pushing himself deep inside with one stroke.

Stretched around him, Elle couldn't imagine a more exquisite sensation.

That was until he moved.

His grip on her hips tightened as he thrust, plunging into her. Elle's sensitized skin registered every whisper of his breath, rough scrape of hair, glide of sweat slicked flesh.

And she only wanted more. She needed it like she needed her next breath.

Eirik lifted his head to stare at her, his breath hot on her cheek. She'd never felt so utterly possessed. As if he took everything while giving everything of himself at the same time.

Her world went blinding white, shattering into glittering shards. For a moment she floated in a sea of bliss then somewhere in the distance Eirik's groan drew her back to earth. The flood of heat deep inside her triggered another orgasm. Gentler but no less powerful, it rippled through her body until she was left languid and boneless.

She blinked until her eyes were able to focus on his face again. "Eirik...that was..." There were no words.

Slumped against her, Eirik sighed. He reluctantly rolled to his side after a long moment. "Amazing. Incredible. Extraordinary." As if he was unwilling for them to be separated, he tugged her until they were facing each other.

Dragging his lips up her neck, he drew a sigh from her. So responsive. Though satisfied, his fatigued body fluttered back to life at the sound. That he hungered for her again after having the latest in a series of mind-blowing interludes with Elle was both intriguing and troubling. He pushed aside all the thoughts.

For the time being, he would be content himself just lying skin to skin with Elle.

She was an enigma. After what had happened to her with Henning, Eirik would have thought she'd be wary of getting entangled in another relationship.

Relationship? Where did that come from?

Eirik halted the idea. This wasn't a relationship. It was just sex. A great vacation. That was all.

So why did he want to know more about her? Why were most of his thoughts of late about Elle?

That he'd even opened up to her was somewhat puzzling. She was just so easy to talk to. Elle didn't judge. She didn't criticize. She listened. Commented. Let him know that what he had to say mattered to her.

Elle was smart and beautiful. Talented and sweet. And, oh, so sexy. He ran his hand over her side. If there was a perfect woman for him in the world, Elle was pretty damned close to being her.

And just what the hell was he going to do about that?

His first instinct was to make sure she stayed with him. Whatever it took. He wasn't beyond a little coercion to get what he wanted. What would she want? What did she want? Eirik could provide her with whatever she wanted and needed. If he did have the ability now, then he would find a way.

The conversation they'd had earlier on the beach flashed through his mind and his heart flopped a little when he recalled that she felt that she'd never had a choice in anything. Not until now.

He wasn't about to take that away from her.

And he wanted her to choose him. To come to him of her own accord. To want to be with him.

From all accounts Elle wanted this to be a temporary arrangement. Hadn't she been saying so this entire time? But her words on the beach...

He might have made up his mind that she was the one for him, but Elle probably wasn't the type to make a decision like that in a matter of days. Or at all, after the disaster that had been her last relationship.

There was nothing he to do besides hope she would fall for him, too.

"What are you thinking?"

He met her gaze. "Nothing."

"Really, because you looked really lost there for a moment."

He had felt lost at the thought of not having her in his life. "It's nothing." Though it was the last thing he wanted to do, Eirik put some space between them.

Elle's expression shuttered. He knew it would the moment he moved, when he'd dismissed her question, he'd ruined the moment. He felt her guard going up.

She tugged the sheets around herself. "It's been a long day. I'm going to get in the shower and get some sleep. In my room."

From the look on her face, he was willing to wager that she was going to get as little sleep as he was.

It was on the tip of his tongue to offer to join her, but Elle was off the bed and out of the door like a shot.

Well, he'd screwed that up. Spectacularly.

Eirik slid from the bed and followed. He knew he should give her time, but he wasn't going to let her just walk off like that. She deserved an explanation and his deserved to be heard.

The water was already running when he strode into her room. And he heard her shuffling about on the other side of her en suite door.

While he was tempted to barge straight in, Eirik tempered the urge and knocked. "Elle?"

The silence between that and her reply said volumes.

"Leave me alone, Eirik."

But he couldn't. "I'm coming in."

She greeted him, arms crossed, glaring and gorgeous in her state of undress.

Eirik's body responded. The anger flashing in her eyes, the haughty tilt of her chin, the utter perfection of her nude body…

"Elle—"

"I get it. This is purely physical. You don't have to worry about me getting clingy."

It wasn't Elle he worried would get too attached.

"Elle."

He liked the sound of her name on his lips. The way it rolled off the tongue. How her name alone was balm that soothed the scars to his soul.

Eirik was a goner.

The need to keep her with him rushed through his body. His mind. His soul. He would do it. By whatever means.

"What—" Elle didn't get another word out before Eirik gripped her in his arms and once again picked her up. Kissing her to silence any further protest, he walked into the glass-enclosed shower. He stopped when they were under the spray, letting the water sluice between them. With their bodies slick, he held her to him allowing nothing to separate them.

The slippery press of her breasts against his chest had to be one of the best sensations in the world. Then she shifted so they slid along his skin and Eirik's knees wobbled.

He couldn't get enough of her. Of her body. Of her smile. Her voice.

Elle was essential to him.

Pressing her to the back of the shower freed his hands so he could explore her wet skin. The torrent of sensations that came with the combination of water and Elle caused his head to spin.

When she reached between them to position his cock at her slit, Eirik groaned and thrust. No finesse, no preliminaries. Just giving in to the instinct to get back inside her.

Elle dropped her head back against the wall and let out a beautiful moan as she wound her arms and legs around him, drawing him ever closer.

Needing no more invitation, Eirik rocked his hips to piston himself in and out of her tight body. What he found amazing was that she felt the same desperation for him that he did for her. Everything she did confirmed the fact. Her kisses, the way she clung to him, how she rocked against him in counterpoint. Every sigh and moan. She might believe that this was fleeting, but her body couldn't lie.

This chemistry, this compatibility, was real and rare.

There wasn't a woman he'd ever met that compared to Elle. He needed more of her. All of her.

He had to find a way to convey that to her while giving her little excuse to turn him down. If that meant staying embedded inside her for the foreseeable future, so be it.

Eirik fought his body's impulse to race to orgasm. The desire to show her what it could be like with him if she decided to stay with him.

When she pulsed around him and cried out her climax, Eirik reached for the shower knob and turned it off before stepping out. He wasn't even sure Elle was aware of what was going on until the dazed expression cleared when he wrapped a towel around them. Unable to bear putting space between them, that was as far as he got to drying them off.

Then they were on the bed.

There was a little mewl that might have been a protest from Elle. Instinct told him it was for getting in the bed wet. Not that it mattered, since they would soon burn it away with the heat between them. He would make sure that any other sound to come from her would be inspired by him.

Her sighs and moans spurred him on.

He gazed at her lovely face, flushed from his lovemaking. Eirik wanted to look onto that face more in the future, whether they were in bed or not.

Eirik wanted this to last forever.

Elle's eyes met his and he asked, "Do you ever want this to end?"

She thrashed her head from side to side. "Never."

"You know only I can do this to you."

She nodded.

"Say it."

"Only you, Eirik," she gasped.

Damn straight. Feeling her inner muscles starting to flutter around him, Eirik pushed into her in earnest, needing to come with her. Her breathy confirmation had him so keyed up that it only took a handful of thrusts before they were both trembling and fighting to regain balance in each other's arms.

Knowing only that he didn't have the strength to move but, at the same time, not wanting to crush Elle, Eirik shifted his weight to the side. He took her with him so they'd stay connected.

Elle wasn't sure what just happened. One moment she'd been sated, floating in the bliss of afterglow, then angry and deflated, then she was declaring he was the only one for her.

What was crazier? She meant it.

It was stupid and reckless but totally from the heart. She was in love with Eirik.

Unsure of what to do about her unwitting declaration, Elle let herself stay safe in the cocoon of his arms for a moment longer before the urge to put space between them took over.

Eirik, it seemed, wasn't in any hurry to let go. Even moving his limbs was a herculean feat, so pushing him off was never going to happen. She shoved at him in earnest.

"What's wrong?" His drowsy question rumbled through her.

So many things. Where to start?

"I don't understand what just happened."

He mumbled something incoherent, but she knew he was asking her to elaborate. How could she when she had no idea how to articulate what was going on in her head when she didn't really know? And even if had been a possibility he expected her to talk while he was still inside her?

Eirik shifted and a streak of pleasure raced through her from where they were still joined. He was getting hard again. Elle had to admit his recovery time was impressive. But was that all she wanted out a relationship? A walking dildo? She wanted a man she connected with in and out of bed. Someone smart as well as handsome. Someone to walk through life with and be proud, happy, content.

For the past few days she had that.

Then why did it feel so wrong?

"Elle. Look at me." Eirik cupped her cheeks so that she had no choice but to peer into his eyes. "We'll figure this out."

Would they? They'd only known each other a few days. She was just getting out of a serious relationship and Eirik...what did she actually know about him?

"I can practically hear your mind working." Eirik's eyes hadn't left hers. He studied her openly and was, in turn, open to her and still she wasn't able to read him.

Elle ran her fingers through his hair, toying with a tendril, brushing the silky ends over her chin. "How can you be so sure we can work things out? We know next to nothing about each other. We come from different places, different worlds. All we have is this."

"Have a little faith."

Did she have any left to spend on this relationship? Was what they had even that? What she wanted was to forget about reality for a little while longer. To put aside everything else but pleasure.

Elle hitched her leg around Eirik's hip. "Give me a reason to believe."

Eirik slid his hands down her body to stroke her skin. He cupped her ass holding her to him while he kissed her. Caressing her mouth with his, soft and slow. The mingling of their breaths and the beat of their hearts against each other added to the intimacy of his kiss.

The heat and pleasure that always came with contact with Eirik was there, only this time it wasn't the instant flash of passion but a slinking warmth that was no less all-encompassing. She wound her arms around his neck as he held her in place for his slow but oh-so-deep thrusts. As if they had all the time in the world, he kept the pace slow. The feel of him sliding under her, inside her, inspired music in her mind like he was a musician and she was his instrument.

The brush of their undulating bodies ignited sparks of fire, though unlike the raging infernos they had generated before, there was smoldering heat. Embers blown upon by their movements, by the friction.

The difference in his kisses, caresses, was subtle, but Elle sensed it. The way he dragged her into his thrusts as if he couldn't get deep enough inside her built her orgasm and swelled the emotion threatening to burst her heart.

With one hand gripping her ass, he wound the other around her back, holding her tight against his hard body. The pebbled peaks of her breasts brushed against his chest, grazed by his hair, adding further fuel to the incredible pleasure Eirik built inside her.

He let out a groan when she nipped his bottom lip before sliding her tongue inside his mouth in a pale parody of what he was doing to her. Eirik swiped her tongue with his as he changed the angle of her hips to take him just a tiny bit deeper. Brought him into better contact with her clit.

The wicked glint that flashed in his eyes at her gasp told Elle he knew exactly what he'd done.

The pace remained unhurried, however. Eirik worked her body like a master to a fever-pitch that unleashed a soul-deep orgasm. While it rolled through her, he took her cries into his mouth pumping into her at the same time. Her world shattered. Still, Elle wanted more. She needed to feel him explode inside her.

She surged against him, meeting him thrust for thrust. Elle clawed her nails into his skin. Moments later it was Elle's turn to take his groans into her as he came. The telltale burst of heat deep inside her made her gasp. Elle breathed his name over and over while her body convulsed around him in reaction.

Her heartrate began to slow, the moment so serene, so perfect that Elle didn't think there was a more sublime experience to be had. There was no doubt when Eirik opened his eyes that he felt it, too.

Things had changed between them.

Chapter Eight

Elle stretched, or at least tried to, but found herself half-pinned by a warm body. A very solid, very big, warm body. Sliding away a bit at a time, she tried to slip from the bed but found herself tangled in the sheets. She heated up just thinking about how they'd managed to get the bed clothes so knotted up.

Eirik sighed, wrapping an arm around her and hauling her close again.

Elle lay frozen until his breathing evened out once more.

Knowing he was fast asleep, she took a moment to just look at Eirik. To really study him. In that moment she wished she was a sculptor or a photographer and could do a study of him. Being a musician, she'd say that looking at him — being with him — was something that inspired symphonies. Gazing at him now, she was stirred to write a piece inspired by his lips alone. He slept on his stomach and took up most of the space, obviously. The morning light played on his arms and back, etching some very interesting shadows that had her mouth watering and fingers itching to explore.

Wriggling her legs, she maneuvered the sheet lower until it rode low on his hips. Another kick and his sculpted ass was revealed.

Taking the time to ogle, Elle sighed. How was it every part of him seemed to be carved from stone? Yet despite his size, he had the ability to be so gentle, so tender, then so untamed in turns. She'd sampled both, but wanted more. Elle wanted to see what else she might inspire him to do to her. What she could do to him with her newfound skills and confidence.

If only they had more time.

His words the night before came back to her. He said they'd figure things out but never explained what he thought they needed to figure out or gave her any clue as to the outcome of the scenario going on in his head.

What did she want?

The truth? To live happily ever after with the man that she'd met on this insane trip.

The funny thing was that Greg had been completely eclipsed. All the time she'd spent with him was forgotten and, as far as she was concerned, no longer mattered.

What kind of woman moved from one man to the next like that?

Still, Greg had cast her aside without a second thought to do something despicable for a woman whose one redeeming quality seemed to be her beauty. And Elle believed he had no more interest than she in getting back together. Even if he did, she would never go back to that stale pseudo-life she'd been sleep walking through.

Greg, just like her old self, was best left in the past.

What bothered her was where her future would lie.

That Eirik still slept soundly didn't surprise her. After last night, she was amazed she was awake. The power of his possession, the near desperation to convey…something intense had been on his mind. That much was obvious. Elle had hoped he felt the same way about her that she felt about him, she believed he did, but the words never came.

Did she need them? After everything Elle was sure that Eirik cared about her with the same intensity she felt for him. Him saying a string of syllables in a particular order, something anyone was capable of doing even without emotion, didn't seem to matter.

Licking her lips and contemplating what that might mean, she eased out from under his arm and untangled herself to go and find her phone. The music in her head rang in her mind so clear and loud she was amazed he couldn't hear it, as attuned to her as he was. There was no way she'd go back to sleep now.

She needed to get the melody out before it faded away.

Putting on Eirik's shirt, she padded out to the living room to find her purse and pull out her phone. Tapping on the screen to navigate to the app, she noticed a few missed calls and a stack of text notifications, which she ignored in lieu of making a fresh pot of coffee.

Coffee and music first, then she'd deal with everything else.

Elle had the app open and had filled several bars with notes before the coffee had finished brewing. She added milk and sugar with one hand while continuing to fill the virtual sheets with the music from her head with the other.

She stepped out onto the balcony to look over what she'd written, hearing the music as if it was coming through the speakers. Leaning over the railing, she sipped and continued to write while soaking up the morning sun.

Being so engrossed in the music was wonderful — felt incredible. However, with her senses so occupied, she didn't notice the approach of someone until they were nearly upon her.

It took her a split second longer to realize that it wasn't Eirik.

Clutching the phone to her chest, she whirled around to find Greg staring at her.

"What are you doing here?" Elle glared at him.

He shrugged. "I saw you here, alone, and thought I would say hi."

"Well you've said it, now leave."

Greg only continued to stare at her as if he couldn't believe what he was seeing. Like she was beautiful, shiny and new. He hadn't looked at her like that in a very long time. Not since they'd first met.

Elle tugged the collar of the shirt together, very aware that she was naked underneath. That and she didn't want him seeing her naked ever again. That she didn't want anyone but Eirik seeing what was under the shirt.

"I asked you to leave."

"I just wanted to talk."

Elle grabbed her coffee and her phone closer. "We have nothing to talk about."

"I think we do."

He said it with such certainty that Elle stopped and looked at him. How had she thought he was the love of her life once? Reedy, short, thinning hair. And his voice… Had it always been this grating? Everything about him rubbed her the wrong way now. And to think that she'd been planning on living with this man for the rest of her life.

The relief that that was no longer the case made her knees sag.

"We don't." She gave him a sympathetic smile. "When you left, I thought…I don't even know what I was thinking. But I realize now that you did me a favor. You did us a favor. We wouldn't have worked out."

"You don't mean that." Greg stepped closer and gripped her arms. "Elle, I want you back."

Eirik held the door in a death grip.

When he woke and couldn't find Elle, he figured she got up to make coffee and write her music. She hadn't seemed able to stop writing and that he provided her with the means made him proud. The happiness wilted, however, when he heard their voices. He'd never thought he would walk in on her talking to her ex.

He stood at the entryway and digested what he'd heard. Elle sounded adamant that she didn't want anything to do with her ex. But then Henning had said he wanted her back and there was nothing but dead silence.

Should he make himself known? What Eirik wanted to do was walk out there and twist the little jerk into a pretzel. This, on the other hand, was the perfect chance to let Elle make a choice. She needed to figure out what she wanted out of life without his influence.

"Elle, please let's just talk about things." Greg was talking again. "I made a huge mistake running off with Celina."

Yes, he had. His blunder had turned out to be Eirik's benefit. He just hoped that Greg wasn't great at persuasion. Then again he had convinced Elle that he was the right man for her once before…

Eirik walked onto the deck and was rewarded with a thankful glance from Elle. With a reassuring smile, he let his gaze wash over her. She looked adorable swimming in his shirt. It hung past her knees and it appeared that she had rolled up the sleeves many times just to let her hands peek through. What he didn't like was that he could clearly see the dusky peaks of her breasts, which meant the other man was able to as well.

He strolled over and wrapped an arm around her without once acknowledging Henning. "There you are, Elle."

Pleasure and pride roared through him when she tugged his head down for a kiss then snuggled close.

But when she glared at her ex after doing it, he knew she was just using him to make a point to the other man. The realization deflated him. He had to remember that, for her, this had been about getting revenge.

Eirik had hoped that stellar sex and the bond he thought was being forged between them was real, but he had been deluding himself from the looks of it. Elle was just like every other woman he'd dated.

Using him for her own ends.

He was well aware of Henning staring wide-eyed at him. He'd put on his trousers, but not having his shirt meant he'd foregone it in his hurry to find Elle. Her ex stood a little straighter, but it only accentuated the differences between them.

Eirik put some space between himself and Elle. "Perhaps I should give you two a moment."

"Not needed." Elle gripped him tighter, but her attention stayed locked on Henning. "Just leave, Greg. There's nothing left to say."

Somewhat wilted, Henning only nodded and quickly left the balcony.

"Are you all right?" Eirik struggled to set Elle back not only because he didn't want to, but because Elle seemed determined to stay glued to him.

She nodded, but there was a glint of something in her eyes that, for the first time, he wasn't able read.

Not sure if he wanted to, Eirik made an excuse. He needed space. "I'm going to take a shower."

She tipped her head back and gave him a sultry smile. "I'll join you."

He shook his head, saw the quick flash of disappointment on Elle's face and felt her withdraw from him. "I'm only going to have a quick one then catch up on some calls."

"Oh." She nodded. "Since we're both up, how about I order some breakfast?"

"If that's what you wish."

Eirik turned to leave, but her hand on his arm stalled him.

"Is something wrong?" Her voice was tiny, unsure. It almost made his wince.

"Nothing. Everything is as it always is." Eirik stepped out of her grasp and stalked back through the house.

"Something is obviously bothering you. Are you angry that Greg was here?" She trailed behind him. Her temper had flared if the hardness in her words was anything to go by.

Why wouldn't she just let it go? Or at least leave him alone.

"I just want a shower and to get on with the day."

Elle stepped in front of him. "I didn't invite him over, if that's what you're thinking."

He walked around her, but Elle doggedly followed and jumped in front of him again.

"Eirik. This isn't you."

Her statement lanced through him. "And what would you know about me? For all you know, this is exactly what I'm like."

"No, it's not. What's going on?" For an agonizing second he feared she would cry, but then horrified understanding dawned on her face. "You're trying to get rid of me. That's it, isn't it?"

He shook his head. That was the last thing he wanted to do, which made it all the more reason to get some breathing space. Eirik closed his hands over his shoulder and moved her out of his path. "I think you should go and talk to Henning. Apparently, there's a lot that you need to discuss."

"Fine." She straightened her shoulders and her chin went up a notch. "You don't have to spell it out for me."

Elle skirted around him again and headed straight for the bedroom. By the time he made it there, she had already gotten her dress on and was looking for the rest of her things.

Were those tears?

Dammit.

"Elle…"

She wasn't listening. She strode into her room and started throwing her things into her bag.

Guilt and what felt like stabbing needles of panic assailed him. She was leaving. He wanted space to figure this out, not for her to walk out. "Elle, wait."

With an angry growl, she dropped it all, kicking everything across the room for good measure. Her breathing hitched as she took vicious swipes at the tears on her cheeks. Elle blew past him. Purse and shoes gathered, she shot him a furious glare before storming to the door.

"Elle." Eirik gripped her arms making her look at him.

"Let go of me, Eirik." She refused to look at him as tears slid down her cheeks.

The pain in her voice, the tears streaking her face, gutted him. Knowing that he was the cause of this made it so much worse. He was willing to do anything to make it better. "Just take a breath. Calm down."

Calm down? Calm down? Because she wanted to punch him, she jerked herself out of his grasp and attempted to get away from him. Elle needed to get far away from him. Right now.

She'd known she had been getting in over her head and that this day was coming, but she hadn't imagined it would all come crashing down like this.

Elle fought for breath when he grasped her hand. She fought him, hating that she loved his touch so much. "I need to be anywhere but here right now."

His jaw tightened. "I hate seeing you like this."

"If you'd get out of the way, you wouldn't have to see it."

"Elle."

She forced herself to look at him. "What?"

"Just go talk to him. We can both see he has something to say. And you know you'll only wonder if you don't."

"I have nothing to say to him and I'm not the least bit interested in anything he wants to tell me. All that will come out of him will be excuses and lies, anyway."

"You don't know that."

She held his gaze. "I do. Do you know what it's like to find out that you've been lied to for months? That someone you've been planning on making a life with probably never felt the same way? To have someone just walk out of your life like you mean nothing?"

Eirik flinched. "I can imagine."

"Well, I'm not letting it happen to me again. If you want to end this, just say so."

Eirik licked his lips.

Elle watched, far too interested in watching his tongue and the path it took before disappearing again. It was enough time to know that he wanted to end this and was just looking for a way of letting her down easy. Wanting her to talk to Greg? Did he think that they would smooth things over and they'd go back to that farce of a relationship again?

Was the need to get rid of her that bad?

"You know what? I will go and talk to him." Elle didn't know what prompted her to say it. She had no intention of sharing the same air as Greg any time soon. What she did know about Eirik was that he would relent when he thought he was getting his way and she needed to get out of there before she said something she regretted.

"Wait."

"For what? For you to find a sweet and gentle way of letting me know that our time's up?" She wiped her tears away. She hadn't expected him to try to stop her, but she was so angry it didn't stop her from stuffing her feet into the shoes then glaring at him. "Don't bother."

Flipping her hair over her shoulder, she haughtily strode out of the door.

It wasn't until she was out in the sunshine that Elle breathed a little easier. And realized she had nowhere to go but wander around before returning to gather her things.

Scrubbing her hand over her face, Elle kept walking. At the very least she'd burn off some frustration while coming up with her next move.

It was always going to happen, it was inevitable, and yet Eirik's rejection was worse than anything else she'd had to endure. Not even Greg walking out on her after living together for years had hurt her to the same extent.

Elle batted away more tears. It was what they'd agreed on from the beginning. To think that it would lead to anything more was stupid. It had just been good sex. That was all. To hope for anything else had been silly on her part.

Stifling the urge to just stop and cry, Elle shoved everything deep down. She'd fall apart later. Right now she needed to keep it together. There was no way she was going to cry over any more over a man, especially not where they were able see her.

How had it come to this? She had just wanted a simple life, maybe make some music and share it with the world. Instead, she had been dumped by one man and was left pining for another within the span of what? A week?

She had to get herself together first, then she'd sort out her life. With or without a man, she was going to get through this. She would be fine. More than.

Elle had enough of her song to think about what to do with it next. Not to mention there was much more to follow.

She had a bright future ahead of her and she wasn't going to let a man ruin that. Ruin her.

"Elle!"

It wasn't the voice she wanted to hear calling her name at the moment.

Elle stalked on. "Go away, Greg!"

"Elle! Come on! Stop being so childish!"

That stopped her. She whirled on her heel to turn and stomp over to him. "Childish? Who was the one who walked out of a relationship without a word? Who was the one who was carrying on with another woman? Who left a woman he was supposed to be marrying to traipse to the other side of the world without so much as a warning?"

With each point, Greg flinched and even had the grace to look embarrassed. "I'm sorry about all of that. I really am." He rubbed his clenched fists up and down his thighs. "Can we do this somewhere more private? I just want to talk to you. To explain."

Where else did she have to go? "You do realize that no matter what you say, I'm not getting back together with you, right?"

There was an admiring glint in his eyes when he accepted her words with a nod. "Shall we go back to my place?"

"What about Celina? I doubt she'd like me there."

Greg shrugged. "She stormed out last night. Haven't seen her since."

So that was why Greg had come back with his tail between his legs. Satisfaction buzzed through her at the thought that he might have some idea now that he'd cast her aside for nothing.

He led her into the villa, but not before Elle took a quick glance next door. Eirik was nowhere in sight. Somehow, that made thing worse. They needed to talk. Once she was done here, she'd go back. Maybe if he knew how she felt it would change things. At the very least, purging everything she'd been hiding might make her feel better.

"Elle?"

She turned her glance to Greg. He'd been talking to her and all she'd done was think about Eirik. "Yes?"

"A drink?"

"I'm fine." She wouldn't be here that long. Elle looked around at the villa and noted that it was smaller, less lavish than the one she shared with Eirik. Still, it would have cost Greg a lot more than he had ever been willing to spend on her in the past.

It was insulting that he'd asked her here. A place that he'd procured for another woman.

"Can you just get on with it?" Elle had to get out of there sooner rather than later.

"Will you at least sit down…" He held up his hands when she glared at him. "Sorry. Again." Greg paused and started pacing while he tried to put words together. "That's what I wanted to say. At the heart of things. I know what I did was wrong." He stopped to look her in the eyes. "And I probably hurt you terribly."

He had. In the beginning. When she'd realized what the hell was going on, the hurt had turned to burning anger. Then she'd met Eirik and Greg had been all but forgotten.

She continued to stare at him, willing him to hurry up.

He shuffled his feet before pacing again. "I don't know...I just thought I wanted something else. Excitement. A thrill."

Meaning she was duller than toast to him. "I'm glad Celina gave you that."

Greg muttered something that Elle didn't catch. Whatever it was didn't sound too flattering toward the other woman.

"What was that?" Elle wanted to hear it.

He cleared his throat, his attention locked on his feet. "She used me. Used me, my skills and my connections to get her what she wanted. Only there were things that I just wasn't capable of providing her with..."

"And what's that?"

"Status. Power. But I couldn't be that guy next door."

No, he couldn't. There was no doubt in her mind that Greg was nowhere near the man that Eirik was.

Elle fixated on the mention of his skills being exploited by Celina. Wanting to get his view of what he'd done, she asked, "The skills of yours she used. I'm assuming your prowess with the market?"

He gave her a glum jerk of his head. "When I met her, it was completely by accident. At least I thought so. She was at that meeting turned party I went to with Richardson and the rest about six months ago. That one you had a migraine and bowed out..."

He'd been cheating on her for half a year! Elle bit her tongue to keep from telling him the truth about her head that night. She had faked it so she didn't have to be subjected to another night of forcing smiles which would have led to an actual migraine. "How did she get in on that?"

"She was hanging around with that idiot Claudio. When we started talking we hit it off immediately. Sparks. Fireworks. Whatever you're supposed to feel when you meet someone incredible."

Nothing like the polite smiles of their first meeting then. "Go on."

"Are you sure?"

"Believe me when I say nothing you can tell me will hurt me any more than you already have."

He winced at that. "Anyway, we fell into a...thing. She'd fly into town a couple of times a month and we'd meet up."

That explained his late nights and surprise meetings.

"She told me about this guy she'd dated a few months before who'd tore her life apart and that she wanted to do the same to him. She really wanted to destroy him and he came up in conversation a lot. Celina told me about his family and how they make their money. I suggested a few ideas." He caught her gaze. "As a joke, you know? Then before long she had me convinced that pulling a 'Pump and Dump' was perfectly reasonable." He licked his lips. "That's when the price of a stock is driven up artificially and then quickly sold to tank the prices of the stocks."

Elle was quite aware of what that was given the reports she'd read. She nodded, encouraging him to continue.

"We created accounts and I encouraged clients to buy, etcetera." He shrugged. "Now we're primed to sell quickly and bring him, all of them, down."

He had no idea he'd been found out...

"So what now?" With Celina out of the picture was he still going to go through with it? Or was he hoping that doing so would bring her back? Elle wasn't about to push the idea on him.

A wicked glint glowed in his eyes as he looked at her. "We do it. Me and you."

Elle jaw dropped. He had to be kidding. "What you're doing is illegal."

"Only if you get caught." He waved off her next comments. "Think about it. We'll finally have the money to do what we want. Take off. Get married. See the world. Just like you always wanted to. I can give you everything you ever wanted and more."

This had to be the most animated she'd ever seen Greg in her company. What he said was right. She had wanted to get married and travel, she still did, but the thought of him being the one she did it with was so insanely wrong. And then for him to suggest that he destroy an entire family and the people that relied on the jobs they provided to get the money to do that? And to profit from that to buy her things that were meaningless in the long run?

Revulsion rippled through her.

"Listen to yourself. You used to know right from wrong. What you're doing is despicable. Think about everyone you'll effect. Have you even thought about that?"

"Celina said —"

"I don't care what she said. Have you taken a look at anything for yourself before you got involved? Do you even care? Or has she got you so blinded you don't even realize what you're doing?"

He puffed up, indignant to the accusation. "Of course I do. I'm in complete control. And I should point out it's because I know exactly what I'm doing we're going to get away with it."

"There's no we, Greg."

"Elle…"

"No." There was no way she could defraud Eirik and his family, or anyone else for that matter, and live with herself. What kind of person did that? It was like she saw Greg for the first time. The real him. The little man with a need to prove just how big he was. Had he always been like this? Or was it Celina who'd brought it out in him?

Or had she finally seen the light thanks to distance and Eirik?

"I can't be a part of something like that. You can do what you want." If this was something Greg was determined to do then it only further proved that she had made the right choice in not getting back together with him.

The wind left his sails a little at that. But from the set of his jaw, Elle got the impression that he was still going to go through with it just to prove something to himself. He'd only be digging himself in deeper.

But he wasn't her problem any longer. She had made her point and that was all she was willing to do.

Greg sighed as he looked at her. Really studied her. "You've changed, you know."

She had and Elle knew it. Would it be possible not to after everything she'd been through this past week?

"You've been glowing like you have a spotlight on you or something. Like when I first saw you at that concert. You shone like an angel that night."

And he had blotted out that light over the years.

"I'm guessing that guy, Eirik, was the one to bring it back." He studied her face. "Right?"

When she didn't answer, Greg cocked his head. "You've been crying."

How nice of him to finally notice. "I'm fine."

"What did he do? Did he hurt you?" Greg gritted the words out through clenched teeth. Did he really think that he could take on Eirik?

"Stop pretending you care about me or my honor, Greg."

"Of course I care!"

"Are you sure? Because everything you've done up until now has said the complete opposite."

He clamped his mouth shut.

"If that's all you had to say..." Elle turned to the door.

A clammy hand closed around hers, stopping Elle from walking out. She tugged her hand out of his grasp and rubbed the residue of him off her skin.

"Elle...I know I can't make up for what I did. I truly am sorry." He held her gaze. "Can we at least try to be friends?"

Why on earth would I want to be friends with him? After all this?

Greg kept going.

"You can tell me the truth. Did he hurt you?"

Not in the way that Greg thought. "Let it go."

"Why? If he's hurt you —"

"He hasn't. Eirik's been nothing but kind, caring and generous. The only person who's hurt me is you." Not quite the whole truth but when weighed against one another, Greg's offenses far outshone Eirik's. At least Eirik hadn't gone out of his way to hurt her.

Greg's face darkened. He glowered at her. Stalked closer. "You've fallen for him."

Elle flinched at the accusation in his voice. It was true. She knew feelings had been growing for Eirik since the day they'd met, but she wasn't about to admit it to Greg. "What are you talking about?"

"I can hear it in your voice when you talk about him. See it in your eyes." He prowled the room again, this time like a caged animal rather than a man thinking things over. "I hoped...I thought that the whole thing had been an act. That you'd flown here to get me back and that you and he...were faking a relationship to get back at us."

She held her breath.

"But it's all real, isn't it?" Stunned by the revelation, Greg stopped to stare at her with condemnation. "Did you know each other before? Had this been planned all along? Or did you meet him here and fall into bed with him the moment he beckoned? Tell me, did you wait five minutes after you met him? And to think I once thought you demure."

He was judging *her*? "You left me, Greg. What I have or haven't done since is none of your business."

Greg's jaw dropped. "You really have changed."

"Only because I'm sick of getting used and cast aside by myopic, insecure men." Taking a deep breath, she straightened her spine and looked him straight in the eyes. "I don't think we can ever be friends after this. I'd appreciate it if you gave me a couple of weeks to gather my things from the apartment. After that..." She shook her head.

Defeated, he nodded. "Very well."

"Goodbye, Greg."

Feeling lighter and freer than she had in a long time, Elle walked out of the villa. But instead of taking the path around, she forged her own trail through the sand to where she knew Eirik was.

She would tell him everything and, if he wouldn't listen, she wasn't above getting naked and trying to convince him that way, either.

Elle laughed at what she imagined his expression would be if she did that.

Running her hands through her hair, Elle practiced in her head what she would say. It would be easy. At least that was what she tried to convince herself. She might not know what had been running through his mind that morning, but Elle had to believe that they would be able to sort it all out. That they would figure out a way of making things work.

Her steps slowed when she approached the familiar building and a tall, leggy blonde approached the front door.

Knowing who it was right away, Elle anticipated Celina knocking and Eirik sending her on her way quickly and without discussion.

So when Eirik opened the door and allowed her to wrap herself around him, press her body and lips to his and propel him back into the villa, Elle's mind and body ground to a halt.

Had that really just happened?

Elle forced herself to move but, minutes later, when the door still hadn't reopened and the woman ejected, Elle stopped again.

She had well and truly screwed up, hadn't she? Left the door wide open, so to speak, for Celina to swoop back into Eirik's life.

Had she ever stood a chance? Even if she was in there, she didn't compare to the blonde. All legs and gleaming hair and oozing sexuality. Five seconds with Celina and Eirik would forget all about *her*, great sex or not.

She had hoped that what they had was real and not just in her head. *Guess I was wrong.*

Willing herself not to cry. Elle stared a moment longer, hoping the door would open and Celina would exit.

After several more long minutes, it was clear she wasn't leaving.

How sad would it be to peek through the windows to see what was happening?

Stifling the self-destructive urge, Elle rounded the villa and climbed up the stairs to the balcony to sneak into her room to grab her things.

Thankfully, or perhaps not so thankfully, the place was well built and she couldn't hear what was going on outside her room with any lucidity. In any case, her imagination filled in the gory details with vivid clarity.

She gathered her things. Quick and quiet like a thief in the night, careful to leave everything that Eirik had given her. Taking them would only remind her of her time with him and that wasn't something she'd be able to deal with. It was best just to put the whole thing down to experience and move on.

But the dress…there was no time to change out of it. Her phone, however… She opened the notepad app with a few brisk swipes and tapped out the words 'goodbye' then left it on the pillow on her way out.

With her heart aching, she took one last look at the room then walked out of the door.

Chapter Nine

Eirik had watched Elle walk into the villa across the way with Henning and had to force himself to stay where he was. Not charging over to kick in the door had been the biggest test of his willpower he'd ever endured. She'd been in there too long and his imagination ran riot. Were they still talking? What could they spend so long talking about? Had it segued into apologies and make-up sex?

The speculation and the emotions raging through him left Eirik ragged in mind and spirit. The restraint it took not to do anything but wait required all his concentration. What was Elle thinking? He had wanted her to talk to Henning, but now that she had, Eirik lost his grip on his confidence that she would return to him.

He had taken a mental health break from staring through the window to pace on the other side of the room when there had come a knock at the door.

Elle? Why would she knock? Had he locked it?

He dashed over and tore the door open to find himself accosted by a perfumed blonde octopus. Shocked, he allowed himself to be pushed back into the villa before he managed to regain his footing and shoved Celina off him. "What are you doing here?"

"I wanted to make up with you." Celina pouted, thrusting her breasts into his chest. "I've missed you so much."

Eirik held his arm out, preventing her from getting closer when she tried to embrace him again. "What on earth would make you believe that I would ever get back with you again? After what you did? What you tried to do?" *After I've found Elle?*

She edged closer. "It was all because I love you. I just went a little crazy when I thought you didn't love me back."

"I don't." He took a big step back, propelling her in the opposite direction.

She stepped into him again and purred, "You don't mean that. Our relationship is just complicated. Passionate. We can work things out."

The last thing he wanted to do was work things out with Celina. His concern was on the woman next door meeting with her ex. What he wouldn't give for a pair of binoculars and the curtains to be open right now.

"Eirik…"

And some privacy while I slowly out of my mind. He looked over her shoulder through the window, though he knew he would see nothing.

"Eirik."

"What?"

"You're being rude and not listening to me."

He scowled at her whining. This had to stop. It was apparent that just listening to her gave her hope that there was a possible be a reconciliation.

Eirik placed his hands on her shoulders and squared her up to him. Leaning down, he leveled his eyes with hers so there would be no confusion. "There's nothing you have to say that I would have any interest in listening to, Celina. We are through."

"What if I told you I knew where your new girlfriend is?"

"I know where she is," he grumbled.

Understanding lit Celina's beautiful face. "Oh…now I understand the grumpiness. You're upset because she's passed you up for her ex."

"She hasn't." *Not yet.* There was still hope that she would come through that door at any moment to declare her love for him. He would do the same and they would live happily ever after. "They're tying up loose ends."

Celina sneered. "I never took you for delusional."

He'd never either. But when it came to Elle, he was getting accustomed to acting and thinking in ways he'd never done before.

Eirik needed that in his life. He needed Elle's light. Her love.

And he'd all but pushed her out of the door into the willing arms of that idiot Henning. He had half a mind to walk across the sand, beat down the door before dragging Elle back and spreading her on the bed under him.

Then make sure she never left him again.

But wasn't this what he'd wanted? Eirik wanted her to choose him. He wanted Elle to want to be with him.

Not to be with him because she had no choice or because she was coerced or had nowhere else to go.

Because she loved him as much as he loved her.

But more seconds ticked by, that was becoming less and less like the option she chose.

What the hell did that moron have that he didn't? One thing he knew for sure — Henning couldn't please Elle in bed the way *he* could.

"You've got it bad, haven't you?" Celina's smug grin tore at his already shredded gut. "This must be killing you."

"Why don't you just leave, Celina? I don't want you here."

"You say that now. But what about later when she doesn't come back and you're lonely?" She ran her finger down his arm. "I'm sure I can find a way of taking your mind off her."

Her suggestion made Eirik's skin crawl. He needed Elle. Pure and simple. No one else would do for him. Not after Elle.

"Get out of here, Celina, before I call security."

"What if I told you that I know about something very bad that can happen to your family's fortune? Or that I have the power to make it go away?"

Eirik glared at her. Even what she and Henning were up to paled to Elle walking away. hearing it come from her own mouth, however, was intriguing enough to catch his notice. That she now had his full attention put a gleam in her eyes that he didn't like.

He swallowed his pride. "I'm listening."

Celina smiled. "I've heard a little something from a little bird. It told me that the man you hate so much right now is plotting to do something very devastating to you."

"And why would he do that?"

She shrugged. "All I know is that he's hellbent on taking you down and has the means to do it."

When it came to bargaining tactics, this had to be the worst he'd ever witnessed. Celina was completely unaware that he held all the chips. Interested in seeing where she was going with it, if only to confirm his suspicion, Eirik waited for her to continue.

"I could be persuaded to convince him otherwise."

"You hold that much sway over him?"

Her smile was smug. "I do. Greg has been mine to toy with from the moment we met."

"So why didn't you stop him from what he was doing, if you knew?"

The smile faltered a little now. "I only just found out."

"I find that hard to believe."

"Why would I lie to you?"

There were so many reasons, Eirik couldn't even begin to count them all. "Yes, why would you?"

"Eirik. I don't know how you've got it into your head that I'm one of those conniving, money-hungry women who would grab on with both hands to the first man they saw with money."

Because he knew that's exactly who she was. "So, if you're going to come back to me, why would Henning do anything for you?"

Celina smiled smugly. "Because he'll do anything I ask."

"Just like he did when you put ideas into his head about manipulating stock in Mikkelsen Engineering Inc? I know all about it, Celina."

Her eyes widened and she paled, but she kept herself together. "What? I don't know what you're talking about."

"You can play the fool all you like. I know about it all." It felt like a lifetime ago that he'd come to the island looking for retribution against her. The need to confront her had been a driving force. Now that he was face to face with her, Eirik didn't care. It was all so empty and meaningless without Elle.

"You don't know anything if you think I had anything to do with Greg's plans." Her voice had gone up and the whites of her eyes were a bit more visible. "I had only found out and came straight over to you to tell you."

"And do all your important topics you raced in to discuss come at the end of your conversations tangled with lies and manipulation?"

"Because I thought you might care, just a little, about what I found out for you, you think I'm trying to manipulate you?"

"Because I know you and the gist of the conversation was, I take you back, you make the problem disappear." He held her gaze. "Am I wrong?"

Tears shimmered in her eyes, but they didn't hide the underlying cunning. "Would it be so hard to love me again?"

How many times could he say it? "There was never any love between us, Celina."

Her lip started to wobble. "That's not true."

"It is. Now that I know what you are truly capable of, I couldn't be happier that things never went any farther with us." He was ashamed their relationship had gone on for as long as it had.

"I'm not capable of the things you accuse me of."

Eirik sighed. He didn't want to continue this conversation. It was going nowhere at all. "I have proof, Celina. I know everything. And soon the authorities will too."

Her tears dried up in an instant, but she didn't budge. "You wouldn't dare."

"Wouldn't I? You tried to take down my family, Celina. And for what? Because you think that being with me will somehow make your life better?" Eirik shook his head. "I can tell you, no amount of money will make you happy if you're not with the right person."

"Saccharine bullshit," she scoffed. "So you're just going to tell them everything..."

"I must."

"Then I'll do what I must." Celina narrowed her gaze at him. "I bet your parents would love that, wouldn't they? You making yet another misstep? A big messy scandal. Another disaster with a woman at the heart of it?"

Glad that she'd given up the pretense, Eirik scoffed at her attempt at a threat. The only thing that would hurt him now would be Elle staying with that prick Henning. Eirik didn't give a damn about what anyone else thought. "I think anything involving you can be rolled into one colossal screw-up, that I'm sure they'll just write it off." He'd already headed off their attempt at ruination so she all the raving and menacing was pointless. Nothing would come of it. She'd lost. Not that he cared. There was only one thing that mattered to him anymore. And she was currently ensconced with her moron ex.

Celina pouted and shrugged again.

How had he have wasted time with such a self-involved, vapid creature as Celina? Yes, she was beautiful, but beyond that there was no substance. Just a woman flitting about looking for a good time and a source of cash.

"Celina, just go. I never want to set eyes on you again. If I do, I'll make sure you go to jail for what you've done."

The cat-that-ate-the-canary grin on her face only grew. "You can't."

"Why not?"

"Because that would mean putting your little sweetheart's boyfriend behind bars too. And I think you care about her too much to do that."

Or it would be a perfect way of keeping them apart so he could work on Elle...

Eirik shook off the idea. No. She would come to him out of love or there would be nothing at all.

The all-too-real possibility that Elle wouldn't be coming back slashed through him with icy claws. This couldn't be the end...

His control on its last thread, Eirik glared at Celina. "Get out. I'm not telling you again."

She had the gall to pat him on the shoulder with her perfectly manicured hand. "You'll get over her soon enough and realize that I'm the one you should be with. I'll be waiting." Celina winked, blew him a kiss then walked out of the door.

Celina would be waiting until the sun fell from the sky.

Eirik sat down at the bar, the perfect vantage point to watch the other house, and waited.

And waited.

Elle wasn't coming back.

The hollowness he felt at the core of him was unlike anything he'd ever felt. How? What they had was good. It might have still been early days but he knew in his heart that they were good together. Great together, in fact. She was everything he ever wanted in a woman and if there was anything about him that she didn't like, he would have done whatever it took to rectify it.

But she wasn't coming back. Elle had gone back to her ex without a second thought.

And it hurt.

Maybe he wasn't meant to love and be loved.

That wasn't true. He loved Elle. He loved Elle with his entire being. She returned the emotion. He saw it. Felt it. No woman could give herself to someone like she did and not feel something and the last time they'd made love had been transcendent.

And he'd been the one to ruin it by insisting she talk to Henning.

He had to reverse what he'd done.

Eirik pulled his phone out of his pocket and dialed her number. It had been a stroke of genius to enter it into his phone when he'd replaced hers. In his head, he patted himself on the back while he waited.

A muffled but persistent musical tone rang in the silence.

What the...

He followed the sound to her room. The first thing he noticed was the phone placed on the bed in a way that had to have been done on purpose, then that her bag was gone.

Unnerved, he hung up and went through the closets one by one to find that everything he'd bought her was still there. Would Elle have gone without them?

But the phone?

With a trembling hand, Eirik picked it up and found it unlocked. Swiping away the missed call notification, he found her note.

Two words that tore out his heart.

Eirik pressed the phone against the throbbing ache in his chest. What had he done?

* * * *

The sun rose far too early the next morning. After the amount of alcohol he'd had the night before to lull him into an insensate stupor, it would have been too soon if it never rose again.

Eirik flinched again as he levered himself up from the couch. What were his options? He'd lost. His first impulse had been to storm next door then drag Elle back to where she belonged. With him.

But what good would it do?

She didn't want him.

Eirik wasn't going to beg for her to love him. Either she did or she didn't. It was clear that she didn't because she'd chosen to go elsewhere.

He wanted her to have the freedom to make the choice.

Eirik loved her enough to make that sacrifice for her happiness.

If she was happiest with a man like Henning, so be it.

So he'd gotten drunk for the first time since he and his brothers had gotten into their parents' bar when they had been in their early teens. The vomiting, hangover and haranguing from their father that resulted had left a lasting impression.

Nothing had made him want to break the years of avoiding binging on hard alcohol until now.

What was he doing? He had more control than this.

Disgusted with himself, Eirik picked up the glass and the near empty bottle of Scotch and took them to the kitchen.

She was only a woman.

So why did it hurt so very much that she chose to be with someone else? Why had he stared at her last message to him as if it answered the mysteries of her mind?

Why had she left everything he'd given her?

Eirik scrubbed his hand over his face. He was a mess and it was all over a woman.

A spectacular woman.

Knowing he shouldn't, but unable to stop himself, Eirik turned his bleary, burning gaze to the villa framed in the window.

He needed to get back to reality and as far away from this place — from the memory of her — as possible.

Then movement caught his attention. Did he really want to see Elle with that little crook?

The truth was, he did. If only to see Elle again. It was sad, and pathetic, but it would be the final time he would allow himself such weakness.

Or so he told himself.

Steeling his gut for what he was about to witness, Eirik stepped closer to the window.

For a long moment he saw nothing but Henning. The other man gesticulated in what looked like pleading with someone blocked from his view by their villa.

He shuffled to the side to get a better look.

Feminine hands pointed and waved, but that was the extent of what Eirik could see of the woman.

Hope buoyed in his heart. Perhaps this fight would end things for good between them.

Eirik didn't care how wretched or pitiful it made him look, he would swoop straight in and make sure Elle never looked at another man. He didn't care that she walked out on him. That she had torn his heart out.

He would treat her like the gift that she was.

Eirik watched Henning drop to his knees and sob something that the woman without a doubt ignored because he stayed there, shocked, mouth agape and shoulders slumped in defeat. Even from that distance, Eirik had heard the door slam.

He felt a pang of sympathy for the other man. Eirik knew exactly what it felt like to be rejected by Elle.

Henning looked exactly how Eirik himself felt.

At least, how he had felt up until that moment.

Uncaring of the circumstances that had led to Henning moping outside the villa, Eirik tidied his hair, straightened his clothes and opened the door.

Just in time to see Henning get up and stumble toward him.

He pointed and shouted over the distance. "You!"

Henning was mad at *him*? Eirik would be lying if he didn't smirk a little bit at that. Elle must have come to her senses and sent him on his way.

The lean man stomped over the sand, kicking it everywhere and still pointing an angry finger.

Eirik stood his ground. "What do you want?"

"So smug aren't you? Like you haven't got it all already." He narrowed his murky brown eyes at Eirik. "How long have you known what we were up to?"

The smaller man clenched and unclenched his fists as if he was contemplating throwing a punch. Eirik bit his lip to keep from laughing. He would wager that not only had Henning had never thrown a punch in his life but that Henning knew if he tried, it wouldn't end well.

Henning must have thought better of punching Eirik and instead rubbed his fisted hands up and down his thighs.

"Does it matter? I caught you red-handed. Now if you have nothing else to say…" Eirik didn't care what the other man wanted—only that he would leave already so he could go talk to Elle.

Or he would just go talk to Elle. What did he care what Henning had to say? "You know what? Get out of the way." Eirik pushed past him.

Or at least tried to. Henning refused to be denied.

"No."

So the runt had a spine. Eirik had to admire that, though it was something he begrudged.

"I've been pushed around by guys like you my entire life. Rich pretty boys who think they can do what they want to who they want. And you know what? I'm sick of it." He jabbed Eirik in the chest. "First you use and discard Celina then you do the same to Elle. When does it stop?" His face turned wistful for a moment. "Elle deserves someone better than you. Someone who doesn't hurt her."

Eirik had had enough. "Like you hurt her? Or are you talking about your embarrassing first steps into the criminal world? You think you are better than me? What you have done to her is worse than anything I could imagine."

Henning's face fell. "That's true. I was an idiot. But that doesn't mean I want her hurt any more. She deserves more than a lying, cheating jerk like you."

Eirik pulled himself up to his full height. "I'm not the cheater here." He pushed Henning aside, sick of his whining. Why was he wasting time with him when he should be with Elle?

"Yeah? So what are you doing now?"

Baffled, but not undeterred by the other man's parting shot, Eirik doggedly made his way over to the villa planning what he was going to say. He wasn't above groveling if it meant getting Elle back.

He took a deep breath before lifting his hand to knock.

"I told you to go away!"

Eirik's gut shriveled when he heard the voice.

The door swung open with explosive force but the venomous look on Celina's face morphed into a delighted grin in an instant. "Eirik! I knew you'd see the light."

His head was only just catching up to his gut when Eirik roared the only thing that was thundering in his mind. "Where the hell is Elle?"

Chapter Ten

Elle stepped out of the cab into the cold and wet Vancouver winter day to look up at the apartment building she had called home for the past few years.

The one she would soon be vacating.

There wasn't an ounce of sadness that came from that realization. Not sadness, not regret. Not pain. Nothing.

Just a calm numbness and the strangest sensation that she was watching all this happen to her from a distance. She would trudge on with her life, though all she wanted to do was go back, find Eirik and live out their days in that villa.

A stupid notion if there ever was one. The man didn't care about her one bit. All that stuff about working things out had just been lip service. And she'd been stupid for even listening to him. So what if he was handsome, smart, funny and deliciously wicked in bed? There would be another who would be better for her.

Yeah. She'd just have to keep telling herself that until she believed it.

Eirik had only been in it for the sex. And maybe for a little revenge. What kind of man was so hell-bent on revenge that he'd forget about everything else?

Not someone she wanted to be involved with, that was for sure.

The nagging little voice at the back of her mind reminded her that her damning thoughts about him weren't true. At least not all true.

She knew she had gotten as close to being addicted to sex with him as a person could be. She had been sure Eirik wouldn't be able to disconnect from that altogether, either. What they shared was powerful, sex or no sex. How could anyone experience what they had and not be changed by it? And, yes, revenge had played a part in propelling them on this path, but it had become less and less of a driving force as the days had gone on.

But then he'd pushed her away.

And had torn her heart out in the same move.

"Is something wrong?"

The cabbie's concerned voice broke Elle out of her reverie. "Not at all." She fished out a few bills from her bag and handed them over. It was bad enough he'd looked at her like she was insane when she approached the cab in the shorts and T-shirt she had changed into while on the plane. "Thanks."

Elle trudged into the building, feeling as though she was walking into a tomb. That was what it was, wasn't it? The remnants of her relationship with Greg.

By the time she opened the door, Elle had decided on the majority of what she was going to keep and what would be left behind.

She let the door swing open while she surveyed the space. It wasn't the height of luxury, but it wasn't a bad place. Just plain. Unexciting. Elle had worked to keep it organized and looking good. As she walked past the pictures on the beige walls, she noticed that the photos of her and Greg together were quite old. From the first few months of their relationship. The rest were either images of them on their own or prints of artwork that Greg admired.

The furnishings, the rugs, the plates, the cutlery…he had chosen them all. Elle had either been absent or had deferred to him to make the choice.

Nothing here showed who they were as a couple. She might as well have been another showpiece to go along with the rest.

Why haven't I ever noticed before?

Disgusted with herself, she stalked into the bedroom where once again his tastes reigned supreme. Elle opened the closet and pulled out her clothes—what few of them there were—and slung them on the bed.

Cocktail dresses, gowns, blouses in varying shades and styles…

What struck her was that they weren't her. None of it was.

Nothing in this place expressed who she was.

And she needed to get out of there.

Elle collected the jewelry that had come to her from her grandmother, a few trophies from her early days as a musician, her cello, her laptop…

She stuck her hand into her pocket to grab her phone out of habit. Of course, she found it empty. Cursing her impulse to leave it behind, she made a mental note to check on her files in the cloud of the music she had written while in Antigua. Even if she couldn't retrieve it, Elle was confident she would be able to write it out again. And would if she had to.

Writing... Elle headed back to the closet and searched the shelf on her side for the pristine books of manuscript paper she had put there when she'd first moved in. Finding them, she promptly added it to the small cache she'd gathered.

Aside from the few things she shoved into her bag, some clothes and her cello, the rest...didn't matter.

Her hand brushed the silk of the dress in the bag, reminding her of all the clothes she'd just left behind. The beautiful ones Eirik had bought.

Those had been her.

Refusing to let herself mope, Elle took one last look at her surroundings before pulling the tiny diamond ring Greg had given her out of the pocket in her bag. The plane ride to Antigua when she'd slipped it off felt like eons ago. With a sigh, she slid it onto the breakfast bar. Then she walked out, locked the door, then took the key off her ring and kicked it back into the apartment. No hesitation. No last look.

Once she was outside again, she breathed the cool air. For a moment she just let it settle inside her, let it warm before breathing it out in a cloud. Not feeling the cold, Elle stood there for a while just existing.

With no expectations put on her, no one to answer to, no one to push her, free to go and do what she liked...

Elle turned her face to the sky to grin before it crumbled and she burst into tears.

* * * *

The building the cab pulled up to this time was wide rather than tall and close enough to Chinatown that Elle could smell the dim sum. Her stomach growled to remind her just how long ago it'd been since she'd last eaten. Food would have to come later.

She rang the buzzer and waited.

"Who is it?"

"It's Elle, Angie."

The door immediately buzzed and clicked. "Come up!"

Angie greeted her at her door, bouncing with excitement, her vibrant red hair flitting with her movement. Always chic, her friend looked perfectly put together while Elle was quite positive she looked like a penniless backpacker at the moment.

Angie's smile faded when she got her first glance at Elle.

Rushing to her and taking her bag before wrapping her arms around her, her friend asked, "What happened?"

Elle sniffled. "I took your advice."

She told Angie the whole sordid tale over pizza and a few cans of Coke.

"They're both assholes." Angie tore a bite out of her slice of pizza. "I'm sorry I ever opened my big mouth."

"It wasn't like you pointed a gun at my head." While the whole ordeal had worn out her emotional batteries, it had turned out to change her outlook on things. Eirik would be remembered with affection for that.

Well, not just for that.

"So this Eirik…."

Elle lifted her gaze from the beaten-up coffee table. "What about him?"

"I don't know. After what you told me he was like, he seems like a stand-up guy."

Until I slept with him. "Don't they all seem that way at first?" Elle sighed. "Can we not talk about him?"

She nodded, understanding softening her expression. "Sure. And you can stay here however long you need. My couch is yours."

Elle smiled. "Thanks." She knew her friend meant it even though Elle had no intention of overstaying her welcome. Angie had her own life to live and she didn't need Elle invading it. But seeing that she didn't have much by way of income or anything else at the moment, she had to resign herself to the fact that sleeping on a couch for the next few weeks, maybe even months, was possible.

"I don't suppose you have an in anywhere that might be interested in offering me a job."

Angie lowered her eyebrows and she pressed her lips together in thought. "I'll ask around. I can see if I can get you in where I work. Or there's always coffee shops in the meantime. They're constantly looking for new people." She sighed. "What about your music?"

The subtext being, 'you were someone in the music world before Greg'. Which reminded her. "I actually wrote something while I was gone."

"You did?" Angie took her hands and started bouncing again. "That's amazing! Where is it?" She looked pointedly at Elle's bag.

"In the cloud. I'll show you once I get my laptop out." Elle shrugged when her friend scowled. "It's a long story. I broke my phone when I was there. Eirik bought me a replacement and made sure that there was an app on it to help me write my music since manuscript paper wasn't exactly available."

"Which explains why my texts and calls went unanswered, right?" Angie gave her a sage nod. "So where's the phone now?"

"I left it there with all the other stuff he bought me."

"Like what?"

"Clothes, jewelry, shoes, accessories..." So many beautiful things that only paled in comparison to the man who had given them to her.

"So this guy bought you a new phone and made sure it had everything you needed on it and bought you all kind of stuff that you loved." She waved away Elle's denial. "I can see it in your eyes that the stuff meant something to you. That he means something to you."

Elle shook her head. "It was all an illusion. He bought me all that stuff to help me play the part of his girlfriend. He wouldn't be with someone like me." She waved at herself, "Look at me. What would a man like him see in me?"

"Are you kidding me? You're gorgeous, smart, talented. If he didn't see that he's an idiot. But I'm pretty sure he did, since he didn't need to buy you a phone, though. Or find an app that suited your needs."

"Angie, it wasn't like that. You're just seeing it from outside."

Angie twirled a lock of her hair around her finger before locking her gaze to Elle's. "Seems to me that's precisely what you need to be doing."

"What are you talking about?"

Her friend shook her head. "Tell me about the revenge stuff. How far did that go?"

"There was a lot of touching and kissing when it was possible we'd be seen. We even went to the same restaurant as them one night."

"That's it?" Angie arched an eyebrow at her.

Elle nodded. "Well yeah. We only had a few days there."

"And that's all the vengeance he could be bothered to serve up to a couple who had tried to wreck his life?"

"We didn't have time..."

"What with all the incredible sex that was happening?"

Mouth dry, Elle nodded again.

"Did he talk about the future, Elle?"

"Yes," she croaked. "Sort of. He said we'd find a way to work things out." Elle shook off the ball of dread growing in the pit of her belly. "But he pushed me away. He wanted me to talk to Greg and sort things out. After that I came to my senses and was going to tell Eirik he was the only one I wanted. But Celina had swooped in and he wasn't in any hurry to get rid of her."

"Did you see what went on between them for yourself?"

Shaking her head, Elle stayed silent, not wanting to admit how much of a coward she had been sneaking in and getting her things before slinking back out.

Angie covered Elle's hand with hers. "Barring the fact that his ex turned up, if you ask me I doubt anything happened between them since she sounds like a total bitch and I'd like to think that he's smarter than that, didn't it ever cross your mind that he was giving you the freedom to choose to be with him or not? You said yourself he had a way of making things work in his favor and that he had a bit of a complex thanks to his family. He probably needed to know you wanted him and only him. Maybe this was his way of giving you room to choose?"

Elle sat frozen with shock.

Of course it was. With all her own insecurities, she didn't even consider what he might have been going through. What could have been going through his mind.

Raking a hand through her hair, she turned to her friend. "What have I done, Angie?"

Her friend dragged her into a big hug. "It's not too late."

"After what I did?" Elle knew Eirik felt as though people didn't want just him. He'd made it clear that the women he'd dealt with in the past were all about the money, the status of being with him.

Maybe leaving all the stuff behind would prove that she wasn't like them? She reached for her phone again before she remembered it wouldn't be there.

"I can't even call him." And flying back to Antigua was out of the question. Even if she had the luxury, what were the chances of him still being there?

Where did that leave her?

"Try searching him on the internet? I'm sure there's got to be a listing for him somewhere." Angie grabbed her laptop while Elle tugged hers out of the bag and turned it on.

* * * *

Over the next few days, most of Elle's time was spent searching for a job and a place to stay on top of trying to find a way to contact Eirik.

For a man the news liked to follow, there was surprisingly little about him online that really mattered. At least to her.

Most of it was about his love life. The less time she spent on that the better—and Elle knew it—but she couldn't help but delve into that black hole for a while. He had been right about the crazy stuff that had been posted about him. Most of it, she considered so inaccurate that it was laughable.

They had him painted as a philandering womanizer who went out of his way to antagonize his family with his antics.

From what she knew about him, that were so far from the truth it verged on fantasy. More than half of the photos were of him and various woman. From the expression on his face and his body language Elle figured the women just happened to be there in time for some photographer to conjure up an absurd story to sell their photo.

As she scrolled through the articles, she found a few images of them in Antigua that had her stopping to scrutinize. Some enterprising photographer had captured them wandering the beach, even having breakfast on the balcony at their villa.

The mood in these images was a far cry from the others. They looks they gave each other, the ones he gave her when she wasn't looking and vice versa, showed her a couple absolutely infatuated with each other.

Elle lingered on them a while before moving on in her search to try to find out more about the enigmatic man she'd fallen for.

Eirik's name was linked to at least a dozen or more architectural projects with his family's firm. The knowledge only drove home the fact that she knew so little about him.

Though what little she did was enough. For now. Elle definitely wanted to learn more about him and hoped she'd get the chance to do so.

Reading about his family had been an eye opener. She knew from their time together that he was a man of means. But the vastness of their empire and the speculation of their true worth made her head swim. They were people she wouldn't have spent time with when she was with Greg. Not even her parents would have run in the same circles.

And she'd been lucky enough to have met and spent life altering time with Eirik.

That, at the very least, made her smile.

She had chased every lead she found with emails and even made a few calls but they all led nowhere. It became clear that Eirik was very reclusive, which did nothing to help her with her quest. Elle even tried to reach his brothers through their family's business site.

She got only as far as their secretaries, however, and no one seemed willing or able to help her. It was only fair. She imagined the screening process to talk to anyone beyond was rather strenuous. And who was she?

The one she was speaking to at the moment was no exception. She had gotten through to one of Eirik's brother's offices.

"*Ja, hallo. Jeg lurte på om...du kunne hjelpe meg?*" Elle rattled off the phrase she'd practiced the last few weeks and prayed that the translation program she used was reliable even if her accent wasn't.

A feminine voice replied. "*Selvfølgelig. Hva kan jeg gjøre for deg?*"

Dammit. It was too fast for her to translate. "I'm sorry. Do you speak English?"

"Of course. How can I help you?" The woman hadn't even needed to think about the language swap.

"I need to get in contact with Eirik Mikkelsen. Can you help me?"

There was a pause. "I can certainly try to relay a message."

"I was hoping you to get his phone number?"

The tittering laugh that lilted through the phone set Elle's teeth on edge. "I'm sorry, but that's not possible."

Elle sighed. "Please let him know that Elle needs to talk to him?"

Laughter was still in her voice when she replied. "Of course. Goodbye."

Elle slashed her finger across the screen, ending the call.

She gave her watch a quick glance and closed her laptop with a slap. If she wasn't down enough, now she had to check out a coffee shop for a job. It wasn't much, but at least it was something.

"Angie, I've got to run. I've got an interview at that coffee place on the corner!"

Her friend burst from her room, wide-eyed and winding her hair into a bun while she darted past. "I'm running late too!"

"I thought you weren't working today." Elle stuffed her feet into a pair of boots and waited for Angie to get caught up to run down together.

"Something came up last minute." Grabbing her keys, her friend gave her a smile. "I think it'll be good for you, though."

"You said that last time you had a meeting with your boss." Elle closed the door behind them before they made their way down the stairs.

"This time I'm sure of it."

Elle laughed. "So I should blow off this interview?"

Angie pushed the front door and held it open for Elle before following her out into the gently falling snow. "Maybe you should keep it, just in case."

"I thought so."

Angie gave her a hug. "Don't give up hope. I might be a little late tonight. So don't wait up!"

They took off in opposite directions.

It wasn't strange for Angie to work late, and this past week had been very busy for her friend. From all accounts her boss was quite a taskmaster. The stories she sometimes told were downright crazy. It came as a bit of a relief when each time Angie approached him, she came back with a no. Still, beggars couldn't be choosers. If it didn't work out with the coffee chop, then she'd be back to square one. Elle would take a crazy job over none at all.

She arrived at the coffee shop with time to spare. Shaking off the snow and stomping her boots on the way in, Elle surveyed the shop. It wouldn't be too bad a place to work. It was close to the apartment and had a homey feel to it.

"You must be Elle."

The woman who approached had a wide smile and greeted her with a warm handshake. "I'm Betty."

"Nice to meet you."

Her smile turned apologetic and Elle braced herself for bad news.

"I'm sorry you had to come all this way, but I didn't have a contact number for you. I'm sorry to have to tell you, the position's been filled. My partner hired someone last night."

Elle did her best not to let her disappointment show. "I understand."

"Again, I'm so sorry. Can I make it up to you with a coffee? Some cake perhaps?"

Not what she was hoping for, but Elle managed a smile. "Thank you. A latte would be wonderful."

"Coming right up."

Well, that had been a bust. Elle sat down at the window to stare at the fluffs of snow drifting to the ground like feathers. There were plenty of other places, though. It was just a matter of time before she found a job.

Betty returned with the promised latte, a slice of red velvet cake and a newspaper. "Here you go, dear. Maybe you'll find something in there?"

"Thanks."

Sipping her drink and flipping through the want ads, Elle took a long moment to stare at the street traffic, looking for a face that she knew wouldn't be there.

What if she called the resort in Antigua and explained? She shot that idea down right away. No one would risk their job over a lame story like the one she had to tell. Who would believe that she would be stupid enough to walk out on a man like Eirik?

Sighing, she continued looking for any job she could conceivably get.

Then she stopped.

Cellist needed.

Elle read over the details and only just managed to contain the squeal of excitement. They needed one straightaway and there was to be an audition that night!

If she tracked the producer down, she could try to persuade them to let her have the music and learn it over the rest of the day. With any luck it would be something she would already know, a classical piece. Even if it wasn't, she was a quick study.

Betty walked past her with a small concerned smile. Elle stopped her with a wave of the paper.

"You wouldn't happen to know where this is, would you?" Elle showed her the address.

"That's not too far from here. It's about a twenty-minute walk." She cringed when she looked out at the snow. It had picked up in the past half-hour. "But in this weather…"

"Just point me in the right direction." Elle gave her an exultant hug when she did and darted out into the sidewalk traffic.

She jogged most of the way, energized by the idea of playing again and getting paid for it. The prospect was exhilarating.

But first she had to get it.

When Elle arrived at the building, her feet and cheeks were freezing, but hope and the run had kept the rest of her warm the entire way.

The stone and glass of the building stretched into the falling snow above, but Elle didn't waste time looking at it. She strode into the foyer and straight to the desk.

Minutes later, she was in an office nibbling on her bottom lip preparing her speech while she waited for the producer to come in.

That hardest part about the wait was not pacing. Elle didn't want to get caught looking like she was out of her depth. She needed to look calm, collected and confident that she would be able to do it all.

So, she practiced Dvorak's *Cello Concerto* in her head as she looked at the décor. Placed strategically around the room was expensive art. Pieces she knew Greg would have been salivating over. Greg even had a print of the painting hanging over the chair behind the desk. The furnishings were big, wood and masculine. They complemented the dark, powerful feel of the room well. The occupier of the space wanted others to know who was in charge. She saw no personal photos on the desk, however. But Elle knew, from visits to Greg's office, that not all men displayed things like that.

She let her gaze drift to the window, but the view outside was drab and obscured by snow. On a clear day, she would have wagered that the view would be spectacular.

"Ms. Suttikul?"

The deep voice startled Elle. Heart beating like hummingbird's wings, she whirled to face the door. There stood a handsome man in a well-tailored suit. His dark hair was cut and styled, his strong jaw clean-shaven. His eyes were what struck her the most. She'd never seen eyes like Eirik's before yet this man's had a warm honey color very close to his. He even had a similar build to Eirik's.

Shaking off the notion, Elle put it down to her superimposing the man she missed over him. As good-looking though he was, Elle couldn't help but compare him to Eirik and find him lacking.

Still, his broad smile put her at ease. "Derek Hunt."

Elle smiled. "A pleasure."

After a quick clasp of her hand in his, he motioned her to sit at the desk while he circled it to take his seat on the other side.

"I understand you're here for the cellist position."

She nodded, her smile widening. "I am. I'm confident that I can fulfill the role perfectly."

He sat back in his seat. "Even on such short notice?"

Elle ran the tip of her tongue over her bottom lip. "I'm sure I can do it. Especially if it's a classic piece that I've played before." He started to say something else, but Elle kept going, not wanting to give him a chance to turn her down. "Because the ad is still running, I believe that you feel you haven't found the right person. I'm telling you that I am. If you give me this chance, I'll prove it."

The nod he gave her was slow and only came after a long study of her face. "Very well."

Elle took the folder that he handed her.

"All the information you need is in there. We'll see you at the Queen Elizabeth Theatre at nine."

"Thank you. I won't let you down." She shook his hand, doing her utmost not to start jumping and squealing in joy. "See you tonight."

Elle flew back to Angie's apartment on a happy cloud.

She kicked off her boots and tossed her jacket onto the couch before pulling out the music and beamed at what she saw.

The *Prelude* from Bach's *Cello Suite No. 1*. Her favorite piece of music.

Could things get any better?

There was one thing that would. But what was the likelihood of Eirik showing up out of the blue?

She took a deep breath. One thing at a time.

Elle tied her hair back into a bun and found a suitable chair which she set up in the middle of the room.

Retrieving her cello, she pulled it from the case and, as if she had last done it only yesterday, started her warm-up.

Chapter Eleven

At eight-forty-five, Elle stood in the aisle with her cello ready and waiting for someone to tell her where she should be.

Wanting to look at best, she wore the red silk dress that Eirik had bought her and had spent a little extra time getting ready. With her hair pinned up in a chignon, her makeup dramatic to match the dress, her confidence was at an all-time high.

She had imagined that she would be a part of an orchestra or perhaps some other people who wanted to listen in. But there was nothing but the stage and a bright spotlight aimed at a chair which stood next to a microphone. Behind them, the curtains were drawn.

"Ms. Suttikul. Lovely to see you again." Derek Hunt approached with the same welcoming smile. "And right on time."

This was it. Blood rushed through her ears as she forced a smile. "Hello, Mr. Hunt. Where do you need me?"

He waved to the stage. "I thought I might hear you play first before we take this any further."

That made sense. If she was a train wreck, they wouldn't waste their time.

She gave him what she hoped looked like a confident nod. "Just give me a minute to set up."

His smile was genial. "Would you like some help?"

She shook her head. The weight of her cello was a comfort. Something she hadn't realized she missed so much. "I'm fine, thank you. If you'll give me a moment?"

"Of course. Take all the time you need."

"Thank you." Elle hefted the instrument and headed on stage. Aware of him watching her, she put the case down, took off her coat, set up and got comfortable.

"That's a lovely dress."

Elle smiled. It really was. Just wearing it boosted her belief in herself. Knowing who had given it to her made it even more dear.

He stood tall and crossed his arms, poised to judge. "Ready?"

Taking a slow breath, she nodded. "I am."

He crossed his arms and nodded. "In your own time."

Closing her eyes, Elle played.

She poured her every emotion, her entire heart, into the music. All the love, the longing, the misery. It was all there plain for anyone who cared to listen.

And it freed her.

By the time she lowered her bow, Elle knew she had given a world-class performance. If he couldn't see that, then she was better off playing elsewhere.

She opened her eyes to see Derek applauding and the impressed expression on his face looked genuine. "Excellent. That was absolutely beautiful."

Her throat was too tight as she waited for his judgment. Elle only managed a stiff nod.

Still smiling, he held his hand out to her. "We have one more audition. So if you'll step down?"

There was someone else? Her happy bubble deflated a little but, confident in her performance, Elle moved her things to the side then stepped off the stage to take a seat in the front row.

The next woman to take the stage was a tall, wiry brunette that Elle recognized to be a premier cellist. The rest of her confidence ebbed away. While she knew what she had done was great, Elle had been rusty going into the performance.

This woman played daily, for sure.

Outclassed and trying not to show her disappointment, Elle sat ramrod straight in her seat.

Of course Derek was going to pick the woman on stage. It was obvious. He'd probably only let her play out of pity.

Still, there was the fact that the whole experience had served to bring back her love of music. This was what she was meant to do.

Brainstorming the possibilities distracted Elle enough to have missed the first few bars of the melody the other woman played.

She forced herself to listen. Maybe she could pick up something?

The music she so fluidly played was haunting… beautiful…and so very familiar…

And hers!

It had taken her a long moment of pure shock before her lungs began to function again. How?

Elle sat stunned that the music she had written in Antigua filled the room. When the curtains parted to reveal an orchestra the same moment they joined in with the cellist, Elle's jaw dropped.

But when she saw the man standing center stage in a tux holding a vivid red rose, Elle's heart threatened to stop altogether.

Eirik's hair had been cut short and his beard trimmed. But there was no mistaking it was him. Her Viking looked a little more tamed but the power in his build — in his presence — was palpable. He was still the most beautiful man she'd ever seen.

As the last strains of the music faded into silence, he bit his lush bottom lip, waiting for her reaction.

Elle gathered up the skirt of her dress and ran up the stairs. Eirik met her at the top, picking her up with ease and wrapping his arms around her.

"I can't believe you did that." There was no way she could feel happier than in that moment. She stared into his eyes, at his handsome face. "I never thought I'd see you again."

Instead of a verbal reply, Eirik let a kiss tell her everything she needed to know. Watching her reaction to her music being played had been incredible, though watching Elle play had been the most mesmerizing thing he'd ever seen. She'd played with her whole heart, her soul. He'd felt every note as if they had been meant for him.

All thought, however, blasted out of his mind when he had her body pressed against his and their lips met. The past few of weeks had stretched into an eternity.

Had it been enough time for her to get over him? He was afraid that he might have taken too long to get back to her but setting everything up had required a little time. And a lot of consideration.

Would she be angry that he looked through her phone for the music? Would she even be impressed? Should he have gone smaller? Bigger? The last few days he'd been sure he was going to go out of his mind second guessing everything in the attempt to make his grand declaration of love perfect.

The dread disappeared and they sank into the kiss. He anchored one hand around her waist while the other tunneled into her hair.

The sensation of her body pressed against his again was something he didn't want to ever go without again.

It wasn't until his lungs burned that he was forced to pull away.

And was rewarded with applause from everyone in the room.

Elle's cheeks flushed the instant the sound registered. Pushing at his shoulders, it was obvious she wanted down.

Eirik held on. "Feel like going to dinner?"

She nodded. "Right after you put me down."

"What if I don't want to?"

"You can't go carrying me the rest of the night."

How about the rest of our lives?

Still, out of deference for her Eirik set her back down on her feet but kept an arm wound around her shoulders.

"I can see why Eirik was inspired to do all this." Derek approached, a smile wide on his face.

Elle bounced her gaze between them. "Eirik told you about me?"

He nodded and punched Eirik in the shoulder. "I refused to help until he did. He wouldn't have told me a thing otherwise."

With them side-by-side, the similarities were amazing. Build, the smiles that were a tiny bit crooked, facial structure, everything but coloring. He could almost see the pieces clicking together in her head. So when she only smiled at his next statement, it wasn't much of a surprise.

On a muttered oath, Eirik scowled. "Elle, meet my brother Nils."

Nils took her hand and shook it. Holding it just a tad too long for Eirik's liking. "I'm sorry about the subterfuge. He insisted it was necessary."

"And my brother wouldn't know a grand romantic gesture if it fell on his head."

His brother had the gall to wink at Elle. "And I completely understand the fuss now. I'm sure we'll be seeing one another again soon."

Eirik cringed as Nils walked away. "I apologize for my brother. He thinks he's got more charm than he actually has."

Elle laughed and shook her head. "It was nice to meet him. You said something about dinner?"

"This way."

Her eyes were luminous when she gazed up at him, as if she still didn't quite believe that he was really there. "Just give me a second to get my coat and cello."

Eirik watched her pack up her things. So beautiful.

The other cellist approached her and they had a quick chat. He could tell Elle was a little starstruck and that made her only more adorable to him. In his opinion, Elle was the most amazing cellist he'd ever heard and to have written that music? Even though it was incomplete, the other woman should have been the one in awe. From the shy smiles, he gathered that she was.

Once her cello was safely placed back in the case, he gently took it from her. His plan was to lead her through the building and to the limo he had waiting. Or at least it had been.

Elle slowed as she reached the entranceway when an arguing couple caught her attention. "Is that Angie arguing with your brother?"

He chuckled. "They've been arguing nonstop since they met a few days ago."

"I knew she had to have something to do with this." Elle gazed up at him. "It must have taken a lot of work."

"It did." And was worth every bit of the effort.

"Is that Betty from the coffee shop?"

He nodded. "Let's just say it took a lot of orchestrating."

She waved at the woman before he led he through the building and to the car. After helping Elle in, he propped the cello against the seat opposite and took the one next to her.

Gratified that she reached for his hand when the car started moving, Eirik sat back and settled in for the ride.

"So what was pushing me to talk to Greg all about?" Elle sat back a bit to look at him, but kept their hands connected. "I have a theory, but I'd rather hear it straight from you."

Well, that was straight to the point. Where to begin? Why not just come straight out and say it? "I wanted you to choose me. To be with me because you wanted to, not because you were on the rebound, not because I coerced you, but because you truly wanted to share yourself with me."

"So pushing me to talk to him was..."

He toyed with her fingers. "I thought there might be some loose ends that needed sorting out."

She pouted and all he wanted to do was kiss those delectable lips again. "And it never occurred to you to just talk to me?"

He shrugged. "Of course I did. It's just everything about you has kept me off-balance." Eirik pressed his lips to her fingertips. "I've never met someone like you before. Never had to deal with emotions like the ones you've brought out in me. I guess I just wanted proof that you wanted me for me. I didn't think what it might have seemed like to you."

"It's the same for me, you know." Elle held his gaze. "I lived in a safe little bubble before I met you. I hadn't realized how constricting it had become, until you came along."

He tugged her closer. "And you don't think that this is just because we've become hooked on what can be only described as out-of-this-world sex?"

She smiled impishly up at him. "Would that be a bad place to start a relationship?"

"When we actually started with something based on revenge, no." He chuckled.

Her expression turned serious. "So what this is...is a relationship, right?"

She really had to ask? Eirik dragged her against him so that he could crash his mouth to hers. It would be so easy to twist and roll her under him...

When Elle pushed him back and slid over him, he wasn't going to say no.

Cuddling her close, feeling her against him... To Eirik there was nothing better. At least for the moment.

Elle kissed Eirik as though her life depended on it.

He had come for her! And not just showed up but prepared an incredible surprise. Elle needed to show him how much he meant to her. How much what he'd done meant to her.

Only, Eirik took her hands in his when she tried to unbutton his clothes.

With a disappointed sigh, he shook his head. "I love where this is going, truly, but we'll be at my hotel within minutes and I'd rather take all night exploring your body."

They were going to his hotel? She licked her lips and nodded. "Okay." They had a lot to discuss as well. Over dinner. Before they got naked.

Tingling with sensation, she eased back and tried to focus her thoughts. A hard task with Eirik so close she still touched him. Smelled him.

She breathed deeply. "I'm sorry for taking off the way I did. But when I saw Celina..."

He looked stunned. "You were there?"

"Yeah, I didn't spend much time talking to Greg. I wanted to get back to you but I saw her go in...then she didn't come out."

Eirik shifted her so that she looked him in the eye. "Nothing happened. I can't imagine what it must have felt like to see." He gave her another gentle kiss. "I'm sorry I ever got involved with a woman like her."

She'd gotten that when she and Eirik first met but hearing straight from him that nothing had happened reassured her tremendously. "So are you going to press charges against them?"

"I've already gotten started on the process."

It was only fair after what Celina and Greg had attempted to do.

"Your family's business is safe?"

He couldn't help but smile at her concern. "Yes."

Then they pulled up at a hotel she'd seen on TV many times in conjunction with the names of stars and dignitaries. Even royalty.

The quick stroll through the lobby and the elevator ride up were a frenzied blur. Elle only retained the sense of decadence. Gleaming hard woods, shiny marble, gilded accents, fresh exotic flowers. The hotel had it all in abundance.

When they arrived at his suite, Elle gasped at the fact that everything was illuminated by a sea of candles. The room alone would have been stunning, but her attention was drawn to the flowers. Huge bouquets of deep red roses sat on almost every surface and perfumed the room with their heady scent.

"Eirik…"

"You don't have to say anything." He took her hand and led her through to the dining room where she was greeted by delicious scents before she even saw the table.

Elle melted. Eirik had recreated the first meal they'd shared.

"I thought we'd start over from the beginning."

Charmed in a way she never thought possible, Elle pressed a hand over her heart. "Just to warn you, I don't know if I can handle any more surprises."

Eirik closed a gentle hand around it and led her to the table. "Only a few more, I promise."

Knees wobbling, Elle poured herself into the chair he held out for her with a grateful smile.

Though she didn't remember having eaten after the coffee at the shop that morning, Elle couldn't eat. Eirik didn't seem too bothered by the food, either, and spent the majority of the time watching her, as if he was afraid she would disappear if he blinked.

"So…" Elle wasn't sure where to begin. There was so much she wanted to say, while at the same time there didn't seem to be the need to. It was clear to her that he was there to be with her. Whether that was for the long run or not, was another matter. But she was content to have him here and now. If that was all they were destined to have, then so be it.

The hope was that whatever they were starting here would last longer.

Was he thinking the same thing? Or was he only going to be with her until the passion burned out?

"Come here." He tugged on her hand until she scooted over to sit on his lap. "You're thinking way too hard."

Elle angled her head to look at him. "Where is this going, Eirik? Are we just fooling ourselves or do you think this is going to go somewhere?"

"It's already gone to a place I've never been. You think I follow women all over the planet? Coordinate elaborate gestures for just anyone?"

Thrilled by his answer, Elle teased him a little. "I really don't know. I've never been with a billionaire before."

"Believe me. You're special."

"I'm glad you think so, because you're amazing, too." Elle hooked her arms around his neck. When her fingers failed to tangle with his new shorter hair, she couldn't stop herself from asking, "So what prompted the new look?"

Eirik tensed. "You don't like it?"

She negated that with a brusque side to side sweep of her head. "I'd love whatever you do with your hair, I just wondered why you did it?"

His muscles relaxed. "You were right when you said I was hiding behind the hair and the beard. It had become a way to keep people away. It was a mask and a deterrent."

"And now?"

"I don't think I need that anymore but I have kept a little because you seemed to like it."

Elle laughed, sliding her hands around to brush her fingers over his neatly trimmed beard. "I do."

Eirik drew her close. "I've also decided on my next ventures."

Oh? Interested in hearing what he was going to do, Elle leaned back even farther to gaze at him.

"As you know, my family is a force in architecture. Modern, soaring constructs that the world marvels over. My opinions on what we could do aren't so popular."

She smiled, understanding where he was going with this. "I take it you're going out on your own."

Eirik smiled broadly. "See? You understand me. There is a glut of buildings left empty around the world that can be repurposed. Why demolish or clear land when they're there, waiting for new life? I've had my eye on one in particular for a while now. An abandoned belle époque multistory in Paris. I envision it as a retro art nouveau hotel."

Enchanted, Elle sighed. "That sounds incredible."

"It will be." He grinned, and she loved how boyish he looked in that moment. "At least that's the hope. I've charmed the investors into thinking so."

"You mean…"

He nodded. "This will be my first autonomous project."

Elle hugged him tight, her heart filled with pride. "It will be amazing."

"I've been in contact with a few hotel chains too including the illustrious Girard Group."

That was a name Elle had heard of before. Her eyes widened. "You have been busy."

"Because I'm setting up a future." He tipped her chin so she held his gaze. "For us. After listening to you play today, I hope you're going to continue with your music. You're incredible whether playing or composing. You need to share your talent with the world."

Her heart filled to near bursting, blotting out the ability to speak.

"Meanwhile, I hope you'll come with me to Paris while I work on the project."

Elated he'd asked, she turned to him. "Paris?"

He snuggled her close. "Do I need to sweeten the deal?"

"No." Elle brushed her lips against his. "You don't."

"Because I brought this with me." He reached into the jacket of his tux and pulled something out.

It was almost slow motion, watching him open his palm to reveal a teal velvet box. His fingers curled around it and pried it open to reveal a glittering diamond ring inside. The huge rectangular gem winked almost like it was enticing her to put it on.

She spared him a quick considering glance before her gaze went back to the ring that blazed with life and promise even in the candlelight. "Are you asking…"

"Yes."

"Then yes." She didn't have to think about it. Didn't need to. Eirik was the man for her.

He continued as if she hadn't answered. "You don't have to accept right away…I know that things have moved incredibly fast with us…" He blinked, registering her words. Eirik stared at her. "You said yes."

"I did." Elle beamed at him.

"You're sure?"

"Absolutely." Elle couldn't be more sure of anything in her life.

Eirik picked her up, winding her around him before he kissed her again. "I promise you will never regret saying yes."

Elle knew she wouldn't.

Epilogue

Five years later

Elle played the final chord and, as the notes of the music echoed away into silence, she opened her eyes to the blinding light.

After what seemed like an eternity, applause erupted in the theater.

She grinned, blinking away the tears that filled her eyes. Playing her music — hearing in reality the mix of pop, rock and classical that had been forged in her mind — gave her a thrill that seemed to get bigger with each performance.

Only a handful of years ago, she'd never imagined she would be writing music. And now here she was on the last night of her tour. After a year of travel that had taken her from Vancouver, to Sydney, to Beijing, to Dubai and all the places between, tonight had been her last night in Vienna. The last night of the entire tour. While Elle was sad she wouldn't be able to explore the city and spend more time in the beautiful Staatsoper opera house, she was excited that she would be getting on a plane in a few hours' time and back to meet Eirik in Oslo.

But first she had to endure an after-party.

She took her bows, joining with the audience to applaud the orchestra that had accompanied her. They were truly incredible. Elle hoped she would work with them all again soon. But right now she had more important things to dwell on.

Her post-performance routine was rushed in lieu of collecting her things. She didn't bother changing, stretching or massaging feet sore from standing most of the performance. At this point she could have forgotten everything but her cello and she wouldn't have cared.

Outside, Elle waded through the crowd, stopping here and there to talk to fans and take photos. That done, she headed straight to her car which waited for her at the curb with her usual driver.

She smiled at Elle and opened the door for her. "I heard your performance was wonderful, Ms. Suttikul."

"I hope it was. It felt great." Grinning, Elle settled back in the soft leather seat and let the excitement of the night wash over her. It had been a triumph. The entire tour had been.

Elle was still amazed at how much things have changed for her over the past few years. And it had all been because she dared to take a step outside of her comfort zone.

She lifted her hand to look at the rings winking at her by the glow of the streetlights as they flew past.

The fire flashing from her engagement ring glittered in time with the ring of tiny diamonds that comprised the wedding band that Eirik had added to her finger a few months after asking her to marry him.

Since then, their relationship, just as their careers, had gone from strength to strength. They spent all the time together they were able, but when it wasn't they kept in close contact via whatever was available. Phone, text, vid chat, email were all put to the test until they were together again. Still, two weeks without being able to touch him whenever she wanted had been agony.

That he hadn't been able to make it to her final performance for this tour had been a let-down, but there would be many more tours. Elle had already finished a dozen more songs for the next album and had ideas for more.

As they arrived at the hotel, Elle got out and took a moment to let her gaze wash over the building glowing in the night. Another one of Eirik's triumphs. The beautiful old building was on its last legs before he unleashed his imagination and architects on it. Now, reservations were some of the most sought after in Europe.

"Good night, Ms. Suttikul." Her driver had appeared at her side with her cello and bag.

"And to you." Elle gave her a smile before picking up her things and heading into the building.

Immense pride in her husband filled her when she strode inside. The décor and design almost had her believing that she had been thrown back in time.

Elle received a deferential smile from the woman at the front desk as she walked into the ornate birdcage elevator. Inside, she swiped her card, allowing her access to the penthouse. She willed it to go faster while it climbed the building. Ordinarily, she enjoyed that

Eirik loved to provide her with the best and brightest of everything. Right now, she just wanted to get to the suite, change and go to the party so that she could get on a plane and back to Oslo.

Luckily the party was being held in the ballroom of the hotel, so she didn't have far to go to and from the event.

Which was excellent considering how exhausted she was.

The doors parted and Elle dashed out to unlock the penthouse door. She placed her cello inside the foyer with care as the lights automatically turned on. The soft illumination revealed a beautiful room that was the next best thing to an actual portal back in time. Elle loved every bit of it.

The suite was the perfect blend of modern convenience and decadent days gone by. She headed to the state-of-the-art sound system to put on some music, preferring that to silence.

Swaying to the throbbing Latin beat, Elle walked through the luxe suite and into the glorious bathroom to turn the shower on, warm and soothing. Pinning her hair up before she undressed, Elle stopped a moment to glance at herself in the mirror. Seeing happiness radiating back at her, Elle smiled on her way to the huge shower. It was reminiscent of the one they had at their apartment, which just made her miss home more.

Alas, there was no time to luxuriate or even ease her sore muscles. There was an annoying twinge in her back that she'd have to get Eirik to look at. From there it wouldn't take much persuasion to get him to pay attention to some other parts of her anatomy as well.

Groaning her frustration, Elle stepped under the water at let it wash over her while she scrubbed away the heavy stage makeup and forced her mind to wander away from thoughts of getting Eirik naked.

She had a gown in mind for the party, but reconsidered it now. Though it was gorgeous, it was just so weighty. Too much when all she wanted to do right now was relax a little. By chance, Elle had brought a few other suitable choices with her. Her favorite sapphire satin dress would be perfect. It was simple in design but the stunning color made up for that.

Elle grabbed the nearest towel to wrap around herself and made her way through to the adjoining closet. She found the dress she wanted without trouble and stepped out into the bedroom to lay it on the bed. Only, she found it already occupied.

Eirik sat against the headboard, bow tie tugged loose, legs crossed at the ankles and an impish smile on his face. "I was wondering how long it would take you to notice me."

Elle dropped the dress and jumped onto the bed and into the waiting arms of her husband. She pressed her lips to his with a happy little scream. Eirik kissed her back as though it'd been years since he'd seen her. She knew he'd missed her as much as she'd missed him.

She drew back only enough to speak. "I thought you weren't able to make it tonight."

He unpinned her hair to tangle his fingers in it, his eyes on her all the while. The love and pride shining there added to the warmth flooding her heart. "Nothing could keep me away from your last performance for this tour."

"So you were there?"

"Of course. And it was spectacular. My parents thought so too. They're waiting at the party with your parents, by the way. We had hoped to catch you afterward but you were in quite a rush," he teased.

Elle was delighted that Eirik's relationship with his parents had changed for the better over the past few years like had hers with her own. Eirik was more contented while his mother and father were elated that he'd taken his talents and made something of himself. There was no one prouder of him than she was, however.

But right now they would have to wait. Elle wanted to reacquaint herself with her husband. "I was in a hurry to meet someone." She slid back and dragged him over her. "But seeing that he's right here…"

Eirik was only too happy to comply. He kept his weight off her however, tangling his legs with hers and using his hands to connect them. "Why the crazed rushed to get to me?" He found his way under the towel little by little.

Elle stared up at her beautiful man, trying not to get distracted by the feel of his hands gently caressing her skin. "You're telling me that after two weeks apart you're not desperate to see me too?"

"I never said I wasn't." Eirik glided his hands over her, up her thighs, waist and ribcage. He cupped her breasts for a long moment before sliding one down to rest on her stomach. "But I thought it might be because there's something important you want to tell me?"

With a delighted squeal, she pulled him down for another searing kiss. She grinned at him when he drew back. "How did you know? I only just had it confirmed this morning."

Smiling against her lips, Eirik murmured, "You don't think I know every inch of your body? You've already changed so much. I noticed the moment I saw you on stage. You're glowing."

Breathless, Elle pulled back to study his eyes, his face. "So?"

"You really have to ask?" He brushed his lips against hers as he caressed her stomach. "I'm delighted. Over the moon."

A baby.

A little bit of them both. It had taken them longer than they had anticipated but now that it had happened at long last...

She kissed him again, parting his lips with her tongue to tease and brush against his. As she knew he would, Eirik untucked the towel and ran his hands over her. It was a long time before he pulled back again.

Elle tugged at the buttons on his shirt.

He chuckled. "Don't we have a celebration to attend?"

"We do." Undeterred, she worked the buttons through the holes, one after another revealing the body she'd missed so much.

"I think what you're doing is the complete opposite of getting ready for it, *elskling*."

Elle smirked at him. "I think I'm doing precisely what I need to have the celebration I have in mind, darling."

Laughing now, Eirik helped. "*Jeg elsker deg.*"

Elle knew the words he said by heart now — she'd heard them often enough. She gazed with adoration at the man who'd changed her life. "I love you, too, Eirik. So much."

Want to see more from this author? Here's a taster for you to enjoy!

The Long Way Round: Grind
Kait Gamble

Excerpt

Pride. It was the first feeling Cara Witchai could describe in her chest every time she looked at her elegant, book-three–months-in-advance Thai fusion restaurant. Then it was happiness, fulfillment—and a little more pride.

After four years and too many sleepless nights picking every pattern carved into the polished teak that lined the walls and fine-tuning every item on the menu, the sounds of people dining and enjoying it now filled the restaurant. A complete success, if she was any judge.

Smiling, she turned to the reservations stacked on her screen when she heard the door open. A quick scan told her that there was nothing available, as she'd expected. She recited her well-practiced greeting easily before she even looked up. "Welcome to Dao. Unfortunately, we're all booked up for the evening…"

"I guess I'll just find a hotdog stand then."

The voice immediately set her body humming as she met his electric gaze and megawatt smile. "Jason!"

A quick sidestep of the teak desk and he wrapped her in his strong arms. Inhaling his addictive scent mingled with whatever cologne he wore, she asked, "When did you get in?" She shifted back to look at him. Not that she needed to. She could remember every inch of him in great detail, right from the top of the jagged peaks of his dirty blond hair down to the brand of boxer briefs he preferred to wear under his tailored suits. That sexy groan he made whenever she ran her nails over the hard muscles of his back…

"Not long ago. Came straight over from the airport thinking I could enjoy something from the best restaurant in town, but it looks like everyone else had the same idea." He scanned the bustling room with sky-blue eyes before returning his gaze to her. He let his hand drift down her arm to capture hers. "Congratulations."

Cara squeezed his fingers. "I didn't do it alone. If you hadn't helped me out in the beginning, I'd never have made it this far."

Jason leaned in to peck her on the cheek, before whispering, "Are you kidding me? This is all you."

Heat climbed into her face and settled in her cheeks. It was hard to tramp down the impulse to drag him into her office and tear the suit off that amazing body. Unfortunately, the heat fizzled a bit when she saw the golden head of her best friend and hostess appear at the door leading to the kitchen. Though she did nothing to disturb the diners, Cara could tell something was up from the pinched expression on her friend's face.

Cara gave Jason an apologetic smile. "Duty calls. Go ahead and relax in my office. I'll have Chelsea bring you something."

He kissed her again, this time brushing his lips over hers. "No rush." With a wink, he sauntered off toward the back of the building.

A woman at a nearby table caught Cara's eye and smirked suggestively as she saluted Cara with her wine.

Cara's lips curved as she thought of the wicked things he could do that would warrant such a look. "Oh, you have no idea." With an anticipatory little shiver and a sigh, she headed for the kitchen to see what was going on.

The scene waiting for her in the gleaming white kitchen wasn't unusual, just something she could do without and had to deal with too often.

Her tall head chef stalked the kitchen, growling at his sous chef, Marco, while the wait staff and the rest of the kitchen staff watched on helplessly.

Cara nudged her friend. "What's going on, Chelsea?" All she could make out were the words 'too much', 'imbecile' and 'overcooked'. The rest was a wild blend of Italian and English that was pretty much incomprehensible.

Chelsea rolled her big green eyes. "Daniel is freaking out about his talent being wasted or something."

"What did Marco do this time?" The countless arguments rattled through her head. Could there be anything new to argue about?

"What makes you think it was Marco?"

Cara snorted at Chelsea's attempt at levity. "It's always Marco." Cara eased her way past the small crowd gathered around the two men. Daniel and his sous chef had a complicated relationship that reminded Cara of a lion waiting for a sign of weakness from the alpha so that he could depose of him. Currently the cub and the alpha were circling each other as if they were going to end it right there.

They were the complete opposite of the relationship she had with Chelsea. They had known each other since the second year of university and had been close friends from the moment they'd discovered their shared love of food and science fiction. They had grown apart over the last few years. But, after a disastrous relationship blow-up, she moved back and Cara hired her as a hostess to help out.

Cara turned to Chelsea, not forgetting the promise she'd made to the man waiting. "Jason's in my office. Could you bring him a bottle of the white then take over at the door?"

Chelsea saluted with a grin. "On my way."

One job down, Cara approached the irate chef and ignored Marco for the time being. Brilliant was the only word she could use to describe her chef. Beautiful and a little high-strung would be the next ones that came to mind. But he wasn't unreasonable. "Daniel, calm down."

The dark-haired man tore his chef's hat off his head and whipped it around like a weapon. "I can't take this anymore, Cara!"

She put a hand gently on his shoulder. "What happened?"

He gestured wildly around him. "He's trying to ruin the food! And *my* reputation!"

Marco, who didn't seem to care that he was a head shorter or that he was technically the subordinate, stabbed the air in front of him with his forefinger. "Lies! I was making the tom yum fried rice better!"

Cara put up her hands before things got physical. "Marco, you are *sous* chef. Daniel's in charge. If you want to make changes, you have to run them by Daniel first. And if not him, then me. If I have to say this one more time, I'll have to find a permanent solution." She looked from one to the other, making sure that her point had been made. "Now, there are people outside waiting for the fabulous food this kitchen creates and we aren't going to disappoint them. So, everyone back to work."

Daniel, to his credit, didn't say anything, but gave Cara a nod in thanks before returning to his station. Marco looked annoyed but contrite, so she felt better about leaving them to their own devices. For now.

"You handled that well."

Jason's voice made her turn around.

She shooed him out of the kitchen and back into the office. "You learn to deal with it when it happens every other week. I was insane to put them in the same kitchen. Separate, they are amazing. You'd think together they could learn to be spectacular."

Cara closed the door quietly behind them, trying to get her mind off kitchen politics. All thoughts fled when Jason closed his strong hands on her waist, spun her around and pushed her back against the hard wood, enveloping her in his embrace.

"I can think of two other people who are spectacular together," he rasped against her neck between gentle nips. "Think your staff can handle a few hours without the boss?"

"They can." It was more a question of if the boss could handle being away from the staff. But with the type of persuasion Jason was using, it was a miracle she managed to get those two words out, let alone worry about anything else.

Capturing her hands in one of his, he pressed them above her head, leaving her defenseless against his lips, his tongue, his teeth and the clever fingers of his free hand. As much as she'd love to jump him immediately, she had something else planned.

"My apartment would be better."

"Here." He tugged down the already low front of her dress and closed his hot mouth over the exposed nipple, laving it with his tongue before drawing back and smiling wickedly. "Now." He lifted her, wrapping her legs around his waist, leaving her open so he could grind himself against her.

"Jason..." She moaned. What was left of Cara's resolve was rapidly evaporating, so she made one last attempt. "We'd have all night if we go back to my apartment. No disturbances. And we'd have a bed."

He groaned mid-lick of her collarbone. She could feel the tension thrumming through him as he weighed the options. Jason nipped her neck, slowly moving back down to her breasts, lingering at one then the other long enough to make her start to question the wisdom of waiting. Then, finally, he hummed in acquiescence. "Let's go. I've got a car waiting outside."

Released from his grasp, Cara almost crumpled boneless to the floor. Jason anticipated it and caught her against him again as he righted her clothes and his. "I'll be outside." After another biting kiss, he buttoned up his jacket, hiding his very evident erection then he was gone.

Cara's head reeled and her senses clamored for more. It was always the same between them. Since they'd first met in college, their chemistry was combustible. It was so good that they'd kept in touch over the years, though it wasn't just the mind-blowing sex that kept them coming back for more. No one else seemed to get her the way he did and vice versa. Only the topic of forever never came up, which was just fine with her. But now this was his third visit in the past two months. Cara knew he was a busy man and that showing up the way he did had to cost him. So then why? Things were fine the way they were before, when he showed up randomly. She actually preferred it.

But he was here now and she was going to enjoy it.

She straightened her dress and ran her fingers uselessly through her hair. It was pointless. She could change into a completely new outfit right now, but one look at her and anyone with eyes would see what they'd been up to. Cara fiddled anyway. She needed to take a moment to catch her breath and slow her pulse.

Once her knees had stopped wobbling, she casually made her way to the front of the restaurant where Chelsea manned the phone.

With a knowing smirk, she asked innocently, "Heading out early tonight?"

Cara ignored the leer. "You think you can handle things without me for the rest of the night?"

"You know we can. You need to take a break. And if the look on the face of your man is anything to go by, you're in for one hell of a break."

There was no question of that.

Chelsea shook her head. "I don't know why you just don't snatch him up. Take him off the market before someone else does."

"It's not like that." She hated trying to defend their arrangement—even more, trying to define it. It was what it was, and she liked it that way.

Her long-time friend wasn't done. "All I know is you two haven't been able to keep your hands off each other since we were first years. And now he blows in here once every few months and for those few days, you look like the happiest woman alive." She crossed her arms. "Tell me I'm wrong."

Cara didn't know what to say. She knew that she enjoyed his visits. Looked forward to them, even. She didn't realize they made her happy enough for everyone to notice. "I'll see you in the morning."

"Nope. You're taking the weekend off."

"Chelsea, I can't." Guilt stabbed at Cara's gut, not only because she was the boss but also because she knew what Chelsea had been through the past few months.

"You can and you will. We're more than capable of dealing with anything that comes our way. If something comes up that I can't handle, I'll call you." Chelsea narrowed her eyes. "And if you're worried about the other stuff that I don't want to talk about, don't be. I'll be fine. Besides, work will do me good."

"Promise?"

"Promise. Now go lock yourself away with that man. Have enough fun for the both of us." Her friend grinned lasciviously.

Twist my rubber arm. Cara knew they could handle themselves but she just liked to be on top of things. Apparently, this weekend she was going to be on top of something much more pleasant than inventory and spats between her staff. "I guess there isn't much else to say. I'll see you Monday."

The shrewd curve of her friend's lips was almost enough to make her cringe, but thoughts of being skin to skin with Jason burned away the embarrassment with a flush of excitement.

She nodded at Chelsea and walked out into the cool evening air. As he said he would be, Jason was waiting for her, casually propped up by a sleek black limo. Without a word, he took her hand, helped her in then followed to settle next to her.

Cara's entire nervous system buzzed with anticipation. Sitting barely a breath apart, their thighs brushed whenever the car's turns shifted them but that was enough to send shockwaves of sensation through her.

A side-glance at him gave her the impression that he was completely unfazed by the contact. That was until she reached his tense jaw and clenched hands.

The privacy partition was up between them and the driver, so there wasn't much chance of being seen or heard.

Cara shifted closer and nipped the rough ridge of Jason's chin on her way up to his ear. "What are you waiting for?"

In a flash, he dragged Cara into his arms and, with a twist, flipped her beneath him. "You have no idea how much I've missed you."

She wriggled against his very impressive erection. "Oh, I think I have an idea."

He pressed harder against her so she could feel every inch of him. "I think we should play this my way."

Cara loved letting him have his way. She'd give just as good as she got in return—which, from his reaction, he enjoyed as much as she did.

"Oh, really?"

Jason grinned slyly as he slowly skimmed his hands up her legs, her dress traveling up with his hands. "How about we play a game?"

"What kind of game?" Cara hooked a leg around his hip.

The car swerved around a corner, the movement crushing them closer together as he dropped his mouth to her neck. "I want you to stay as quiet as you can."

Cara could hear her pulse in her ears, feel it in her throat. "While you do what?" His touch inched upward and she knew exactly what he had in mind.

He slipped his fingers past the scrap of silk that was her panties and eased into her, eliciting a gasp then a moan as he began to move them. When she mewled, his movement ceased. "Not a sound or I stop."

Nodding, she raised her hips, trying to get more pressure, more contact. More Jason.

Chuckling, he crooked his fingers, sending waves of pleasure racing through her. Cara stifled a gasp by biting his shoulder.

Hissing a long breath, Jason gave her a slow smile. "Like that?"

Like it? She could barely breathe. "More."

Jason obliged increasing the friction until Cara's body hummed like an instrument under the fingers of a master musician. The pleasure was too intense, too much, too fast. Her orgasm slammed into her without warning.

He captured her scream in a searing kiss as he eased her back to reality.

By the time her vision cleared and the roaring in her ears calmed, Cara realized that the limo had stopped. Jason stared down at her, his eyes intense and his breathing as labored as hers. She had to smile. He was losing his control.

Cara kissed him, biting his lower lip and soothing the sting with her tongue. "Your turn."

Sign up for our newsletter and find out about all our romance book releases, eBook sales and promotions, sneak peeks and FREE romance books!

About the Author

Kait was born and raised in the wilderness of the Pacific Northwest and started writing to entertain herself during the long winters as a child. Insatiably curious with a love of learning new things, she's picked up many random skills including three languages and two martial arts. After travelling three continents (the other four are on her bucket list), she settled in England with her family where she spends most of her time cultivating her daughter's love of reading and writing, scribbling ideas on every available scrap of paper, and trying out dialogue on her cat.

Kait loves to hear from readers. You can find her contact information, website details and author profile page at https://www.totallybound.com